2000

To Phillip,

From Grandpa &
Grandma

This book
belongs to

_____

My First Collection of Stories, Rhymes and Songs

This is a Dempsey Parr Book
First published in 2000

Dempsey Parr is an imprint of Parragon
Parragon
Queen Street House
4 Queen Street
Bath BA1 1HE UK

Copyright © Parragon 2000

Printed and bound in Indonesia
ISBN 0 75500 005 6

My First
Collection of Stories,
Rhymes and Songs

DP
DEMPSEY
PARR

Contents

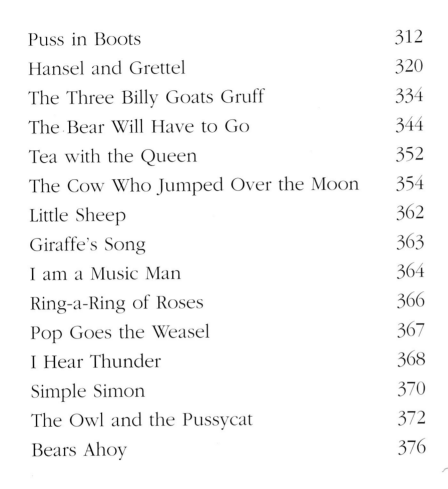

Introduction

This *First Collection of Stories, Rhymes and Songs* is packed with family favorites to give hours of pleasure and fun. There are classic nursery rhymes, fairy stories and songs, traditional fables and tales all retold in an easy to read style, together with contemporary stories with a wealth of exciting and endearing characters. To add to the fun, there are action songs with drawings to explain all the actions! Every page is bursting with colorful illustrations to delight young readers everywhere.

Round and Round the Garden

Round and round
the garden,
Like a teddy bear;

One step, two step,
Tickle you under there!

Round and round
the haystack,
Went the little mouse.

One step, two steps,
In this little house.

Circle palm

Walk fingers up arm

Tickle!

ROUND AND ROUND

ONE STEP, TWO STEP

TICKLE!

If You're Happy and You Know It

If you're happy and you know it,
Clap your hands.
If you're happy and you know it,
Clap your hands.
If you're happy and you know it,
And you really want to show it,
If you're happy and you know it,
Clap your hands.

If you're happy and you know it,
Nod your head, etc.
If you're happy and you know it,
Stamp your feet, etc.

If you're happy and you know it,
Say "ha, ha!", etc.
If you're happy and you know it,
Do all four!

Twinkle, Twinkle, Little Star

Twinkle, twinkle, little star,
How I wonder what you are!
Up above the moon so high,
Like a diamond in the sky.

Ride A Cock-Horse

Ride a cock-horse to Banbury Cross,
To see a fine lady upon a white horse,
With rings on her fingers and bells on her toes
She shall have music wherever she goes.

Knick Knack Paddy Whack

This old man, he played one,
He played knick knack on my drum.
With a knick knack paddy whack, give a dog a bone,
This old man went rolling home.

This old man, he played two,
He played knick knack on my shoe.
With a knick knack paddy whack, give a dog a bone,
This old man went rolling home.

This old man, he played three,
He played knick knack on my knee.
With a knick knack paddy whack, give a dog a bone,
This old man went rolling home.

This old man, he played four,
He played knick knack on my door.
With a knick knack paddy whack, give a dog a bone,
This old man went rolling home.

This old man, he played five,
He played knick knack on my hive.
With a knick knack paddy whack, give a dog a bone,
This old man went rolling home.

The Frog Prince

There was once a king who had but one daughter. Being his only child, she wanted for nothing. She had a nursery full of toys, a pony to ride and a wardrobe bursting with pretty dresses. But, for all this, the princess was lonely. "How I wish I had someone to play with," she sighed.

The princess's favorite toy was a beautiful golden ball. Every day she would play with her ball in the palace garden. When she threw the ball up in the air, it seemed to take off of its own accord and touch the clouds before landing in the princess's hands again.

One windy day the princess was playing in the garden as usual. She threw her golden ball high into the air, but instead of returning to her hands, the wind blew the ball into the fishpond. The princess ran to the pond, but to her dismay the ball had sunk right to the bottom. "Whatever shall I do?" wailed the girl. "Now I have lost my favorite toy." And she sat down beside the pond and cried.

All at once she heard a loud PLOP! and a large green frog landed on the grass beside her. "Eeeuugh! Go away you nasty thing!" screamed the princess.

To her astonishment, the frog spoke to her. "I heard you crying," he said in a gentle voice, "and I wondered what the matter was. Can I help you in any way?"

23

"Why, yes!" exclaimed the princess, once she had got over the shock of being addressed by a frog. "My ball has sunk to the bottom of the pond. Would you fish it out for me?"

"Of course I will," replied the frog. "But in return, what will you give me if I do?"

"You can have my jewels, my finest clothes and even my crown if you will find my ball," said the princess hastily, for she was truly eager to get her favourite toy back.

"I do not want your jewels, your clothes or your crown," replied the frog. "I would like to be your friend. I want to return with you to the palace and eat from your golden plate and sip from your golden cup. At night I want to sleep on a cushion made of silk next to your bed and I want you to kiss me goodnight before I go to sleep, too."

"I promise all you ask," said the girl, "if only you will find my golden ball."

"Remember what you have promised," said the frog, as he dived deep into the pond. At last he surfaced again with the ball and threw it on to the grass beside the princess. She was so overjoyed she forgot all about thanking the frog – let alone her promise – and ran all the way back to the palace.

That evening the king, the queen and the princess were having dinner in the great hall of the palace, when a courtier approached the king and said, "Your majesty, there is a frog at the door who says the princess has promised to share her dinner with him."

"Is this true?" demanded the king, turning to the princess and looking rather angry.

"Yes, it is," said the princess in a small voice. And she told her father the whole story.

"When a promise is made it must be kept, my girl," said the king. "You must ask the frog to dine with you."

Presently, the frog hopped into the great hall and round to where the princess was sitting. With a great leap he was up on the table beside her. She stifled a scream.

"You promised to let me eat from your golden plate," said the frog, tucking into the princess's food. The princess felt quite sick and pushed the plate away from her. Then to her horror the frog dipped his long tongue into her golden cup and drank every drop. "It's what you promised," he reminded her.

When he had finished, the frog stretched his long, green limbs, yawned and said, "Now I feel quite sleepy. Please take me to your room."

"Do I have to?" the princess pleaded with her father.

"Yes, you do," said the king sternly. "The frog helped you when you were in need and you made him a promise."

So the princess carried the frog to her bedroom but as they reached the door she said, "My bedroom's very warm. I'm sure you'd be more comfortable out here where it's cool."

But as she opened the bedroom door, the frog leaped from her hand and landed on her bed.

"You promised that I could sleep on a silk cushion next to your bed," said the frog.

"Yes, yes, of course," said the princess looking with horror at the froggy footprints on her clean, white sheets. She called to her maid to bring a cushion.

The frog jumped on to the cushion and looked as though he was going to sleep.

"Good," thought the princess, "he's forgotten about my final promise."

But just as she was about to get into bed, he opened his eyes and said, "What about my goodnight kiss?"

"Oh, woe is me," thought the princess as she closed her eyes and pursed her lips towards the frog's cold and clammy face and kissed him.

"Open your eyes," said a voice that didn't sound a bit like the frog's. She opened her eyes and there, standing before her, was a prince. The princess stood there in dumbstruck amazement.

"Thank you," said the prince. "You have broken a spell cast upon me by a wicked witch. She turned me into a frog and said the spell would only be broken if a princess would eat with me, sleep beside me and kiss me."

They ran to tell the king what had happened. He was delighted and said, "You may live in the palace from now on, for my daughter needs a friend." And indeed, the prince and princess became the best of friends and she was never lonely again. He taught her to play football with the golden ball and she taught him to ride her pony. One day, many years later, they were married and had lots of children. And, do you know, their children were particularly good at leapfrog.

The Town Mouse and the Country Mouse

Once upon a time there were two little mice. One mouse was very grand and lived in the town but the other was quite different. He was a Country Mouse. He lived under the roots of an old oak tree in a small hole lined with straw and dry grass. He slept on a scrap of sheep's wool and wore a brown waistcoat he had made himself from an old grainsack.

"How lucky I am to live here," the Country Mouse said to himself. "I must invite my cousin to come and share my cosy home," but when the smart Town Mouse arrived, he looked about the little hole in dismay. What a shabby home! The Country Mouse laughed and led him to a table piled high with food.

"I have prepared a special meal," he said excitedly. "A cob of corn, fresh hazelnuts and rosy red rosehips."

But the Town Mouse wrinkled his nose in disgust.

"I cannot eat this food," he protested. "You must come and stay with me and discover what real food is like." So the next day the Country Mouse returned with the Town Mouse to his home in the big, busy city.

"This is what a home should be like," said the Town Mouse proudly as he led the Country Mouse from room to room. "I like soft carpets and comfortable furniture. There are no leaves or mud here."

Soon they were hungry. "Follow me," said the Town Mouse, "but there will be no rosehips or hazlenuts on the menu!" he added with a twinkle in his eye. The little Country Mouse gasped when he saw the wonderful spread laid out on the large dining table.

"This is *real* food," cried the Town Mouse. "Let us begin!" but as soon as he scampered across the floor two large dogs came bounding into the room, barking fiercely and the Country Mouse drew back in terror.

"I'm going back to my home!" he told his cousin. "You may sleep on a soft duck-down mattress under a satin quilt while I have only a scrap of wool for my bed. You may wear a red velvet coat with gold buttons while my clothes are patched and darned. You may feast on roast beef and chocolate cake while I live off the nuts and berries of the hedgerow. You can enjoy the excitement of the town if you wish but give me the plain and simple life any time!"

AND THE MORAL OF THIS STORY IS:
BETTER A POOR AND CAREFREE LIFE
THAN A RICH AND WORRIED LIFE

BRER RABBIT AND THE WELL

Brer Rabbit was hard at work in the garden with Brer Fox, Brer Raccoon and Brer Bear. The sun was hot and he was fed up..

"Oo,oo! I gotta sharp thorn in my paw!" he cried, pretending he had hurt himself, then off he skedaddled mighty quick to find a nice cool place to rest. Pretty soon he came across a well with a bucket hanging down into its shady depths.

"That looks like the very spot for me," he said to himself and into the bucket he jumped. Well, the bucket didn't stay still! No, it dropped like a stone to the bottom of the well. Poor Brer Rabbit didn't have much time to think about where he might be heading because all of a sudden the bucket hit the water with a loud splash and then Brer Rabbit knew that he was in a real fix.

Back in the meadow Brer Fox had stopped work. He knew Brer Rabbit was up to no good and decided to follow him. He hid behind a tree and watched as Brer Rabbit stopped by the well, and when he saw him jump in the bucket he could hardly believe his eyes!

"That must be where Brer Rabbit keeps all his money hidden," he said to himself, "or maybe he's found a gold mine!"

Slowly he crept to the well and peered over the edge. There wasn't a sound to be heard. Down at the bottom of the well poor Brer Rabbit sat hunched up in his bucket, hardly daring to twitch a whisker. Suddenly a loud voice echoed down the well.

"Howdy, Brer Rabbit," called Brer Fox. "What are you doing down there?" Brer Rabbit thought hard.

"I'm fishing," he replied. "There are some mighty fine fish down here, Brer Fox. Why don't you come and get some for yourself?"

Brer Fox licked his lips hungrily. He liked fish.

"I might just do that," he called out. "But how do I get down there?"

"That's easy," cried Brer Rabbit. "Just hop into that bucket you see at the top of the well and it'll bring you straight down for sure." Soon Brer Fox was in the bucket and heading for the bottom of the well.

But what he didn't realise was that as he went down, Brer Rabbit was going up! Halfway down the well, they passed one another.

"Guess this is the way of the world, Brer Fox," laughed Brer Rabbit. "Some go up and some go down!" Then Brer Fox knew that the Rabbit had got the better of him and there was absolutely nothing he could do about it! When he reached the top of the well, Brer Rabbit hopped out of his bucket and ran straight to Brer Bear and Brer Raccoon.

"Brer Fox is down the well!" he cried, "and he's making our water all muddy." Soon the other animals were hauling the poor Fox up and he was really mad! But that Brer Rabbit just laughed and laughed to think how well he had tricked his friend!

BARNEY THE BOASTFUL BEAR

Barney was a very boastful bear.

"Look at my lovely soft fur!" he would say to the other toys. "See how it shines!"

Barney loved to talk about himself. "I'm the smartest toy in the playroom!" he would say. "It's a well-known fact."

He didn't know that the other toys all laughed about him behind his back.

"That bear thinks he's so smart," growled Scotty Dog. "But he isn't smart enough to know when everyone's fed up with him!"

"He'll learn his lesson one of these days," said Molly Monkey, and sure enough, that is just what happened...

44

One hot summer's day, the toys lazed in the warm playroom. "Wouldn't it be lovely if we could go for a walk outside," said Rag Doll.

"We could have a lovely picnic in the woods!" said Old Bear.

"Even better, we could go for a drive in the toy car first!" said Rabbit.

"But none of us is big or clever enough to drive the toy car," said Rag Doll, sadly.

"I am!" came a voice from the corner. It was Barney. He had been listening to them talking.

"I can drive the toy car. And I know the best place for a picnic in the woods," he said.

"We've never seen you drive the car," said Rabbit, suspiciously.

"That's because I drive it at night, when you're asleep," said Barney. "I'm a very good driver, in fact."

"Ooh, let's go then!" cried Rag Doll. And in no time they had packed up a picnic and were sitting ready in the car.

"Er, I don't feel like driving today, actually," mumbled Barney. "It's too hot." But the others

were not interested in hearing excuses, so rather reluctantly Barney climbed into the driver's seat and started the engine. You see, the truth was, Barney had never really driven the car before, and he was scared. But he wanted to show off, so he pretended to know what he was doing.

Off they set down the garden path. "Toot, toot!" Barney beeped the horn as he turned the little car out into the country lane, and soon they were driving along, singing merrily

All was going well, until Rag Doll suddenly
said, "Hey, Barney, didn't we just miss the
turning for the woods?"

"I know where I'm going," said Barney,
crossly. "Leave it to me." And he made the
little car go faster.

"Slow down a bit, Barney!" called Old Bear,
from the back seat. "My fur is getting all ruffled."
He was starting to feel anxious.

"I don't need a back seat driver, thank you,"
said Barney, with a growl, and made the car go
even faster. By now the others were starting to
feel scared, but Barney was having a great time.

"Aren't I a wonderful driver!" he chuckled. "Look – no hands!" And he took his paws off the steering wheel. Just then they reached a sharp corner. The little car went spinning off the side of the road and crashed into a tree, tipping all the toys out into the ditch!

They were a bit dazed, but luckily no one was hurt. They were not pleased with Barney though. "You silly bear!" said Rabbit, crossly. "We could have all been badly hurt!"

"We'll have to walk home now," said Rag Doll, rubbing her head. "Where are we?"

Everyone looked at Barney.

"Don't ask me!" he said, quietly.

"But you said you knew the way!" said Old Bear, indignantly.

"I was only pretending," said Barney, his voice trembling. "I don't really know how to drive, and I don't know where we are!" And he started to cry.

The other toys were furious with Barney.

"You naughty boastful bear!" they scolded. "Now see what trouble your boasting has got us into!"

The lost toys walked through the dark woods all night long, clinging together in fright as shadows loomed around them.

They had never been out at night before. Then just before dawn, they spotted the little house where they lived, and crept back into the playroom.

What a relief it was to be home again!
Luckily their owner had not noticed they were missing, so she never knew what an adventure her toys had been having while she was fast asleep. She often wondered what had happened to her toy car though.

As for Barney, he was very sorry for the trouble he had caused. After a while the other toys forgave him, and from that day on he never boasted about anything again.

THE LITTLEST PIG

Little Pig had a secret. He snuggled down in the warm hay with his brothers and sisters, looked up at the dark sky twinkling with stars, and smiled a secret smile to himself. Maybe it wasn't so bad being the littlest pig after all...

Not so long ago, Little Pig had been feeling quite fed up. He was the youngest and by far the smallest pig in the family. He had five brothers and five sisters and they were all much bigger and fatter than he was. The farmer's wife called him Runt, as he was the smallest pig of the litter.

"I don't suppose little Runt will come to much," she told her friend Daisy, as they stopped by to bring the piglets some fresh hay.

His brothers and sisters teased him terribly. "Poor little Runtie," they said to him, giggling. "You must be the smallest pig in the world!"

"Leave me alone!" said Little Pig, and he crept off to the corner of the pig pen, where he curled into a ball, and started to cry. "If you weren't all so greedy, and let me have some food, maybe I'd be bigger!" he mumbled, sadly.

Every feeding time was the same — the others all pushed and shoved, and shunted Little Pig out of the way, until all that was left were the scraps. He would never grow bigger at this rate.

Then one day Little Pig made an important discovery. He was hiding in the corner of the pen, as usual, when he spied a little hole in the fence tucked away behind the feeding trough.

"I think I could fit through there!" thought Little Pig, excitedly.

He waited all day until it was time for bed, and then, when he was sure that all of his brothers and sisters were fast asleep, he wriggled through the hole. Suddenly he was outside, free to go wherever he pleased. And what an adventure he had!

First, he ran to the henhouse and gobbled up the bowls of grain. Then he ran to the field, slipped under the fence, and crunched up Donkey's carrots.

He ran into the vegetable patch and munched a whole row of cabbages. What a wonderful feast! Then, when his little belly was full to bursting, he headed for home. On the way he stopped by the hedgerow. What was that lovely smell? He rooted around until he found where it was coming from — it was a bank of wild strawberries.

Little Pig had never tasted anything so delicious. "Tomorrow night, I'll start with these!" he promised himself as he trotted back home to the pig pen.

Quietly he wriggled back through the hole, and soon fell fast asleep snuggled up to his mother, smiling contentedly.

Night after night Little Pig continued his tasty adventures, creeping out through the hole when the others were sleeping. He no longer minded when they pushed him out of the way at feeding time, as he knew a much better feast awaited him outside. Sometimes he would find the farm dog's bowl filled with scraps from the farmer's supper, or buckets of oats ready for the horses. "Yum, yum — piggy porridge!" he would giggle, as he gobbled it up.

But as the days and weeks went by, and Little Pig grew bigger and fatter, it was more of a squeeze to wriggle through the hole each night.

Little Pig knew that soon he would no longer be able to fit through the hole, but by then he would be big enough to stand up to his brothers and sisters. And for now he was enjoying his secret!

Morag the Witch

Morag was just an ordinary witch – until the day she enrolled for a course of advanced spell casting at the Wizard, Witch and Warlock Institute of Magic. For that was where she met Professor Fizzlestick. Now Professor Fizzlestick was a very wise old man indeed. Morag, on the other hand, was a very vain young witch who didn't know as much as she thought she did. She could turn people into frogs if they really deserved it, and do other simple spells like that, but she still had a lot to learn. The problem was, Morag thought she was the most perfect little witch in the whole wide world.

Morag's adventure started on her very first day at school. At the beginning of the day, after all the young witches and wizards had made friends and met the teachers, they were called in one by one to talk to Professor Fizzlestick.

"Now, young Morag Bendlebaum, I taught both your mother and your father," said the professor in a very serious voice, "and a very fine witch and wizard they turned out to be, too. So, what kind of witch do you think you are going to be?"

Without giving this any thought at all, Morag blurted out, "I'm better than my parents, and I'm probably better than you!"

This answer surprised even Morag, for although she thought this was true, she didn't actually mean to say it.

"Don't be surprised by your answers," said Professor Fizzlestick, "there is a truth spell in this room, and whatever you truly believe you must say. And I have to say that you appear to have an enormously high opinion of yourself. Why don't you tell me what makes you so very good?"

"I'm clever," said Morag, "and I'm good, and I'm always right."

"But what about your dark side?" said Professor Fizzlestick.

"I'm sorry to disappoint you," replied Morag quite seriously, "but I'm afraid I simply don't have a dark side."

"Well in that case I would like you to meet someone very close to you," said Professor Fizzlestick with a smile on his lips.

Morag looked over to where Professor Fizzlestick pointed, and was startled to see on the sofa next to her… herself!

As Morag stared open-mouthed with astonishment, the professor explained that if, as she believed, she was without a dark side, then there was absolutely nothing to worry about. "If, however," he continued, "you have deceived yourself, then I'm afraid you are in for a few surprises."

With that the professor dismissed them both from the room and told them to get to know each other. As Morag and her dark side stood outside the professor's room, Morag's dark side jumped and whooped for joy. "At last," she cried, "I'm free. I don't have to sit and listen to you telling me what's right all day; I don't have to keep persuading you to choose the biggest slice of cake before your brother – in fact, I don't, I repeat **don't,** have to do anything that you tell me at all."

So saying she broke into a run and rushed down the corridor, knocking over chairs and bumping into other little witches and wizards along the way. Morag was horrified. She would have to follow her dark side and stop her from causing trouble. Morag chased after her dark side and finally caught up with her at the chocolate machine. "Don't eat all that chocolate," cried Morag. "You know it's bad for your teeth and will ruin your appetite for lunch!"

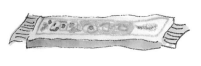

"Tsk!" scoffed her dark side. "You might not want any chocolate but I certainly do!" And with that she ran off once more, dropping chocolate on to the freshly polished floor as well as pushing a big piece into her mouth.

Just then, the bell sounded for lunch. Although Morag felt she ought to find her dark side, she also knew that the bell was a command to go to the dining hall, and she mustn't disobey it. Morag sat down to lunch next to her friend, Topaz. She was just about to tell her what had happened, when she saw that Topaz was not eating her vegetables! Morag scolded Topaz for this, and gave her a lecture on eating healthily.

Topaz stared at Morag in amazement, then peered closely at her. "What's happened to you?" she asked.

Morag explained what had happened in Professor Fizzlestick's office, and then declared, "And you know, it's the best thing that has ever happened to me. I thought I was good before, but now I'm even better. I never want my dark side back again, but we must find her and lock her up so that she can do no harm."

Topaz agreed that they must find her dark side, but secretly hoped that she and Morag would be re-united. Morag wasn't Morag without her dark side.

After lunch, Morag went for her first lesson of the afternoon. When she walked into the classroom she discovered her dark side already there, busy preparing spells! Morag's dark side had already prepared a 'turning a nose into an elephant's trunk' spell and a 'turning skin into dragons' scales' spell and was just finishing off a 'turning your teacher into stone' spell!

Morag suddenly heard a trumpeting noise from the back of the classroom. She turned to find that the wizard twins, Denzil and Dorian Dillydally, had both sprouted huge gray trunks down to the ground where their noses had been. Morag rushed over to her dark side to make her change them back, but before she could reach her she tripped over a creature crouching down on the floor. It looked just like a dragon and it was wearing a purple and white spotted dress last seen on Betina Bumblebag. Morag's dark side was casting spells all over the place. "Oh, why doesn't the teacher stop her!" cried Morag to Topaz.

I'm sure you've guessed by now. Nice Miss Chuckle was entirely turned to stone from head to foot!

Just then Professor Fizzlestick walked into the classroom. Morag pointed to her dark side, still making spells at the front of the classroom.

"Lock her up immediately," Morag begged the professor.

"I'm afraid that you are the only one who can do that," said the wise old man. "The two of you are inseparable and you need each other. Without your dark side you would be unbearable and without you she is dreadful. Have I your permission to lock her back inside you?"

Even though Morag didn't want any part of her dark side back, she agreed reluctantly. Her dark side instantly disappeared, and Morag felt... wonderful! Oh, it was so good to be back to normal, to be basically good, but occasionally mischievous.

"Thank you," said Morag to the professor. "I think I've learned something very valuable today."

"There is good and bad in everyone," replied the professor, "even the most perfect of witches."

Morag blushed when she remembered what she had said earlier that morning, but she was so relieved to find she was normal that she really didn't mind. Morag and Topaz went back to the classroom to undo all the bad things Morag's dark side had done, but on the way they both felt a huge urge for a snack, so they stopped at the chocolate machine first!

Jimbo Comes Home

Jimbo the circus elephant was snoring away in his cage one night when he heard a strange noise. At first he thought it was part of his dream. In his dream he was walking across a hot, dusty plain while in the distance there was the sound of thunder.

All at once Jimbo was wide awake. He realised that he was in his cage after all and that what he thought was the sound of thunder was the noise of his cage on the move. Now this worried him, because the circus never moved at night. He rose to his feet and looked around. He could see men pulling on the tow bar at the front of the cage. These were strangers – it certainly wasn't Carlos his trainer! Jimbo started to bellow, "Help! Stop thief!" But it was too late. His cage was already rumbling out of the circus ground and down the road.

Eventually, the cage passed through a gate marked 'Zipper's Circus' and Jimbo knew what had happened. He had been stolen by the Zipper family, his own circus family's greatest rivals! Jimbo was furious. How had the thieves got away with it? Surely someone at Ronaldo's Circus must have heard them stealing him? But Jimbo waited in vain to be rescued.

The next morning, the thieves opened up Jimbo's cage and tried to coax him out, but he stayed put. In the end, after much struggling, they managed to pull him out. Once he was out of his cage, he took the biggest drink of water he could from a bucket and soaked his new keeper! He refused to cooperate, kicked over his food, and when he appeared in the circus that night he made sure he got all the tricks wrong.

"Don't worry," said Mr Zipper to Jimbo's new trainer, "he'll just take a little while to settle down. Soon he'll forget that he was once part of Ronaldo's Circus." But Jimbo didn't forget for, as you know, an elephant never forgets.

The other animals in Zipper's Circus had all been stolen from other circuses, too. "You'll just have to get used to it here," said one of the chimps to Jimbo. "It's not so bad really." But Jimbo decided he was going to try and escape.

One night, a mouse passed by his cage. "Hello," called Jimbo mournfully, for by now he was feeling very lonely, and no-one had cleaned his cage out for days.

"Hello!" said the mouse. "You don't look very happy. What's the matter?" Jimbo explained how he had been stolen and wanted to escape back to his own circus. The mouse listened and then said, "I'll try to help." So saying, he scampered off and soon he was back with a bunch of keys. Jimbo was astonished. "Easy!" said the mouse. "The keeper was asleep, so I helped myself."

Jimbo took the keys in his trunk and unlocked the door to the cage. He was free! "Thank you!" he called to the mouse, who was already scurrying away.

Jimbo's first thought was to get back to his own circus as fast as possible. However, he wanted to teach those thieves a lesson. He could hear them snoring in their caravan. He tiptoed up, as quietly as an elephant can tiptoe, and slid into the horse's harness at the front. "Hey, what do you think you're doing?"

neighed one of the horses, but Jimbo was already hauling the robbers' caravan out of the gate and down the road.

So gently did he pull the caravan that the thieves never once woke up. Eventually they reached Ronaldo's Circus. Mr Ronaldo was dumbstruck to see Jimbo pulling a caravan just like a horse! Mr Ronaldo walked over to the caravan and was astonished to see the robbers still fast asleep. He raced to the telephone and called the police, and it wasn't until they heard the police siren that the robbers woke up. By then it was too late. As they emerged from the caravan scratching and shaking their heads they were arrested on the spot and taken off to jail. "There are a few questions we would like to ask Mr Zipper regarding the theft of some other circus animals, too," said one of the police officers

Mr Ronaldo, and Jimbo's keeper Carlos, were both delighted to see Jimbo back home again. And Jimbo was just as delighted to be back home. Then Mr Ronaldo and Carlos started whispering to each other and began walking away looking secretive. "We'll be back soon, we promise," they said to Jimbo. When they returned, they were pushing Jimbo's old cage. It had been freshly painted, there was clean, sweet-smelling straw inside, but best of all there was no lock on the door! "Now you can come and go as you please," said Carlos.

And Jimbo trumpeted long and loud with his trunk held high, which Carlos knew was his way of saying, "THANK YOU!"

Little Cottage in the Wood

Make roof with hands

LITTLE COTTAGE

Look through hands

MAN BY THE WINDOW

Hold up fingers

RABBIT RUNNING

Knock fist in air

KNOCKING AT DOOR

Little cottage in the wood,
Little old man by the window stood,
Saw a rabbit running by,
Knocking at the door.
"Help me! Help me! Help me!" he said,
"Before the huntsman shoots me dead."
"Come little rabbit, come inside,
Safe with me abide."

Wave arms up and down

HELP ME!

Point with one finger

HUNTSMAN SHOOTS

Beckon with same finger

COME INSIDE

Stroke hand (rabbit)

SAFE WITH ME

 # I'm a Little Teapot

SHORT

AND STOUT

HANDLE

SPOUT

I'm a little teapot
short and stout,
Here's my handle,
here's my spout,
When I get my
steam up hear me shout,
Tip me up
and pour me out.

STEAM UP

SHOUT

TIP

POUR

76

Okey Cokey

You put your left arm in, your left arm out,
In, out, in, out, you shake it all about,
You do the okey cokey, and you turn around,
And that's what it's all about.

LEFT ARM IN...

Oh, the okey cokey,
Oh, the okey cokey,
Oh, the okey cokey,
Knees bend, arms stretch,
Ra, ra, ra!

Rhyme continues with right arm, left leg,
right leg, whole self.

LEFT ARM OUT...

SHAKE IT ALL ABOUT...

TURN AROUND...

KNEES BEND, ARM STRETCH

77

Dancing Round the Maypole

Dancing round the maypole,

Dancing all the day,

Dancing round the maypole,

On the first of May,

Dancing round the maypole,

What a merry bunch,

Dancing round the maypole,

Till it's time for lunch.

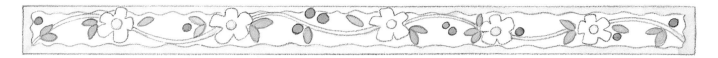

Dancing round the maypole,
Shouting out with glee,
Dancing round the maypole,
Till it's time for tea.
Dancing round the maypole,
Blue and white and red,
Dancing round the maypole,
Till it's time for bed.

Old Mother Hubbard

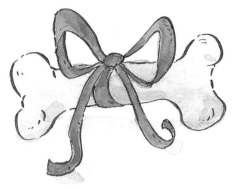

Old Mother Hubbard
Went to the cupboard
To fetch her poor dog a bone,
But when she got there
The cupboard was bare
And so the poor dog had none.

Tom, Tom The Piper's Son

Tom, Tom, the piper's son,

Stole a pig and away he run!

The pig was eat, and Tom was beat,

And Tom went roaring down the street.

The Boy Who Wished Too Much

There once was a young boy named Billy. He was a lucky fellow, for he had parents who loved him, plenty of friends and a room full of toys. Behind his house was a garbage dump. Billy had been forbidden to go there by his mother, but he used to stare at it out of the window. It looked such an exciting place to explore.

One day, Billy was staring at the garbage dump, when he saw something gold-colored gleaming in the sunlight. There, on the top of the dump, sat a brass lamp. Now Billy knew the tale of Aladdin, and he wondered if this lamp could possibly be magic, too. When his mother wasn't looking he slipped out of the back door, scrambled up the dump and snatched the lamp from the top.

Billy ran to the garden shed. It was quite dark inside, but Billy could see the brass of the lamp glowing softly in his hands. When his eyes had grown accustomed to the dark, he saw that the lamp was quite dirty. As he started to rub at the brass, there was a puff of smoke and the shed was filled with light. Billy closed his eyes tightly and when he opened them again, he found to his astonishment that there was a man standing there, dressed in a costume richly embroidered with gold and jewels. "I am the genie of the lamp," he said. "Are you by any chance Aladdin?"

"N… n… no, I'm Billy," stammered Billy, staring in disbelief.

"How very confusing," said the genie frowning. "I was told that the boy with the lamp was named Aladdin. Oh well, never mind! Now I'm here, I may as well grant you your wishes. You can have three, by the way."

At first Billy was so astonished he couldn't speak. Then he began to think hard. What would be the very best thing to wish for? He had an idea. "My first wish," he said, "is that I can have as many wishes as I want."

The genie looked rather taken aback, but then he smiled and said, "A wish is a wish. So be it!"

Billy could hardly believe his ears. Was he really going to get all his wishes granted? He decided to start with a really big wish, just in case the genie changed his mind later. "I wish I could have a wallet that never runs out of money," he said.

Hey presto! There in his hand was a wallet with five coins in it. Without remembering to thank the genie, Billy ran out of the shed and down the road to the candy store. He bought a large bag of candies and took one of the coins out of his wallet to pay for it. Then he peeped cautiously inside the wallet, and sure enough there were still five coins. The magic had worked!

Billy ran back to the garden shed to get his next wish, but the genie had vanished. "That's not fair!" cried Billy, stamping his foot. Then he remembered the lamp. He seized it and rubbed at it furiously. Sure enough, the genie reappeared.

"Don't forget to share those candies with your friends," he said.

84

"What is your wish, Billy?"

This time Billy, who was very fond of sweet things, said, "I wish I had a house made of chocolate!"

No sooner had he uttered the words than he found that he was standing outside a house made entirely of rich, creamy chocolate. Billy broke off the door knocker and nibbled at it. Yes, it really was made of the most delicious chocolate that he had ever tasted! Billy gorged himself until he began to feel quite sick. He lay down on the grass and closed his eyes. When he opened them again, the chocolate house had vanished and he was outside the garden shed once more. "It's not fair to take my chocolate house away. I want it back!" he complained, stamping his foot once again.

Billy went back into the shed. "This time I'll ask for something that lasts longer," he thought. He rubbed the lamp and there stood the genie again.

"You've got chocolate all around your mouth," said the genie disapprovingly. "What is your wish?"

"I wish I had a magic carpet to take me to faraway lands," said Billy. No sooner were the words out of his mouth than he could feel himself being lifted up and out of the shed on a lovely soft carpet. The carpet took Billy up, up and away over hills, mountains and seas to the end of the Earth. He saw camels in the desert, polar bears at the North Pole and whales far out at sea. At last, Billy began to feel homesick and he asked the magic carpet to take him home. Soon he was in his own back yard again.

Billy was beginning to feel very powerful and important. He began to wish for more and more things. He wished that he did not have to go to school – and so he didn't! He wished that he had a servant to clear up after him and a cook to make him special meals of sweet things – and a cook and a servant appeared.

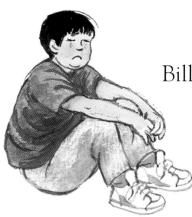

Billy began to get very fat and lazy. His parents despaired at how spoiled he had become. His friends no longer came to play because he had grown so boastful.

One morning, Billy woke up, looked in the mirror and burst into tears. "I'm so lonely and unhappy!" he wailed. He realised that there was only one thing to do. He ran down to the garden shed, picked up the lamp and rubbed it.

"You don't look very happy," said the genie, giving him a concerned glance. "What is your wish?"

"I wish everything was back to normal," Billy blurted out, "and I wish I could have no more wishes!"

"A wise choice!" said the genie. "So be it. Goodbye, Billy!" And with that the genie vanished. Billy stepped out of the shed, and from then on everything was normal again. His parents cared for him, he went to school and his friends came to play once more. But Billy had learned his lesson. He never boasted again and he always shared his candies and toys.

How the Leopard got his Spots

Long, long ago, the Leopard and the Ethiopian lived in a 'sclusively bare, hot and sandy-yellow-brownish place called the High Veldt. The Giraffe and the Zebra lived there too and they were 'sclusively sandy-yellow-brownish all over. But not as sandy-yellow-brownish as the Leopard and the Ethiopian. The Leopard would lie down behind a brownish rock and the Ethiopian would hide behind a clump of yellowish grass and when the Giraffe or the Zebra would come by, they would leap out of their hiding places and give them the fright of their jumpsome lives. Indeed they would!

After a long time the Giraffe and the Zebra learnt to stay away from the parts of the High Veldt that could be hiding a Leopard or an Ethiopian and they began to look for somewhere else to live.

The Giraffe and the Zebra went to the forest. It was quite different from the High Veldt for it was full of stripy, speckly, patchy-blatchy shadows and there they hid safe from harm. After an even longer time (things lived for ever so long in those days), what with standing in the slippery-slidy shadows of the trees, the Giraffe grew blotchy and the Zebra grew stripy.

By now the Leopard and the Ethiopian had grown very hungry and so they asked Baviaan, the wise Baboon, where the other animals had gone.

"They decided it was high time for a change and they have gone into other spots and my advice to you, Leopard, is to do the same." Then the Leopard and the Ethiopian searched the forest but although they could smell them and they could hear them, to their great surprise they found they could not see the animals.

Soon it grew dark, and then the Leopard heard something breathing sniffily quite near him. It smelt like Zebra and when he stretched out his paw it felt like Zebra. So the Leopard jumped out of his tree and sat on this strange thing until morning because there was something about it that he didn't quite like.

Presently he heard a grunt and a crash and he heard the Ethiopian call out.

"I've caught a thing that I cannot see. It smells like Giraffe and it kicks like Giraffe but it hasn't any shape."

"Don't trust it," advised the Leopard. "Just sit on its head till the morning comes, same as me." So there they sat and waited until the sun rose for then the light would show them just what they had caught.

At sunrise the Leopard looked over at the Ethiopian.

"What have you got down your end of the table, Brother?" he asked. The Ethiopian scratched his head.

"Well, it ought to be Giraffe, but it is covered all over with chestnut blotches. What have you got?"

"Well, it ought to be Zebra," replied the Leopard, equally puzzled, "but it's covered all over with black stripes. What have you both been doing to yourselves?"

Then the Giraffe and the Zebra stood up.

"Watch us disappear," they said and they walked off towards some tall bushes where the shadows fell all blotchy and stripy. "This is the way it's done. One, two, three, where's your breakfast?" The Leopard stared and the Ethiopian stared but all they could see were stripy shadows and blotchy shadows.

"That's a lesson worth learning!" declared the Ethiopian. "I'm going to change myself, too. I want to be a nice blackish-brownish color. It will be the very thing for hiding in hollows and behind trees." So he changed his skin then and there and when he had finished he spoke to his friend. "You should take Baviaan's advice, Leopard, and go into other spots, too."

"Very well," decided the Leopard, "but don't make 'em too vulgar-big. I wouldn't look like Giraffe — not for ever so." So the Ethiopian pressed his fingertips all over the Leopard and soon he was covered in spots.

Wherever the Ethiopian's five fingers touched his coat, they left five little black marks, all close together. Sometimes his fingers slipped and the marks got a little blurred, but if you look closely at any Leopard now you will see that there are always five spots — off five fat black fingertips.

"Now you can lie out on the ground and look like a heap of pebbles," said the Ethiopian. "You can lie on a leafy branch and look like dappled sunshine. Think of that and purr!"

And so the animals were very proud of their new coats and were very glad that they had changed. Oh, one last thing. Now and again you will hear grown-ups say, "Can the Leopard change his spots?" I don't think even grown-ups would keep on saying such a silly thing if the Leopard hadn't done it once — do you? But they will never do it again, Best Beloved. Oh no, they are quite contented just as they are.

The Golden Goose
Illustrated by Claire Mumford

Once upon a time there were three brothers. The youngest son was given the name of Dummling and was laughed at by his family and everyone else.

One day the eldest son went into the forest to cut some wood. His mother gave him cake and a bottle of wine and off he went, whistling cheerfully. But he had no sooner set to work than a little old man appeared.

"I am so hungry and thirsty. May I have some cake and wine?" he asked. But the eldest son shook his head.

"Be off with you," he said gruffly. "I will share my meal with no-one." But it seemed the old man was going to get his revenge with the very next swing of the ax for it landed on the eldest son's foot. How he yelled! The next day the second son decided to try his luck and once again his mother gave him cake and wine.

The little old man approached the second son and asked to share his meal, but the second son also refused. He, too, was cut by the next swing of the ax.

The next day Dummling set off for the forest to cut some wood. He was given only bread and water but was happy to share what he had with the little man.

"You are a good boy," said the man, "and if you cut down that tree you will get your reward." Dummling did as he was bid and was astonished to find a goose covered entirely with golden feathers.

"I will go to the city and seek my fortune," Dummling decided. "This beautiful goose will bring me luck." As he strolled along the lane he passed a girl. She gasped to see such a glorious golden bird and stretched out her hand to stroke it. But imagine her dismay when she found that she could not take her hand away! The goose had magic powers and whoever laid a finger on her soon found themselves stuck fast to her feathers.

Before many hours had passed Dummling had collected two more inquisitive girls and a Parson, all stuck fast one behind the other. As they stumbled across the fields they met the Bishop.

"My dear Parson!" he cried. "Have you taken leave of your senses?" and he reached out and caught the Parson's sleeve. Now he, too, was stuck fast and it wasn't long before they were joined by a plowman and a shepherd!

After a time they reached the city and there in the palace lived the King and his daughter. She had never been known to smile and the King had promised her hand in marriage to the first person who was able to make her laugh. Well, when the Princess saw the three girls, the Parson, the Bishop, the plowman and the poor shepherd all falling over one another behind Dummling's golden Goose, she burst into peals of laughter.

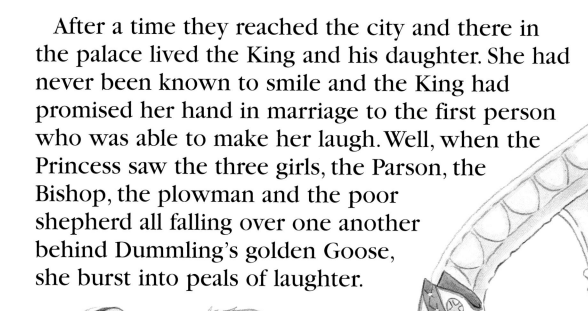

The King came running and Dummling lost no time in asking permission to marry the Princess.

"Hmm," thought the King to himself. "I do not want this raggle taggle boy to marry my daughter. I must set him an impossible task to perform and when he fails, I will be able to refuse him."

And so the King told Dummling that before the marriage could take place he would first have to find a man who could drink a whole cellarful of wine.

Dummling scratched his head and then he remembered the old man in the forest. But when he returned to the glade the old man was not there. Instead, he found a short man with a miserable face.

"Oh, my, I am so terribly thirsty," he moaned. "I have already drunk a barrel of wine but I feel as if I could drain a lake dry!"

"You are just the man I am looking for!" cried Dummling and he led the man to the King's cellar.

The fat man rubbed his hands with glee.

"This is a sight for sore eyes!" the short man declared and soon he had emptied every bottle, keg, cask, and barrel. The King was more vexed than ever. He decided to set another task and this time made it even harder.

"Find me a man who can eat a whole mountain of bread," he ordered, well satisfied that this would indeed prove impossible.

But Dummling went straight to the forest and there discovered a tall, thin man sitting on a log.

"I have just had four ovenfuls of bread for my supper but it has barely taken the edge of my appetite," he complained. Dummling pulled at his sleeve.

"I know a place where you can eat your fill," he said.

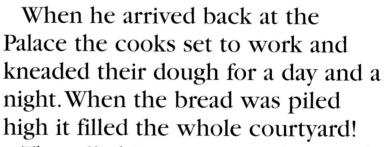

When he arrived back at the Palace the cooks set to work and kneaded their dough for a day and a night. When the bread was piled high it filled the whole courtyard!

The tall, thin man ate and ate and ate and within hours the mountain had become a molehill, and soon there was nothing left at all.

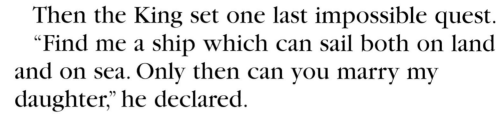

Then the King set one last impossible quest.

"Find me a ship which can sail both on land and on sea. Only then can you marry my daughter," he declared.

This time Dummling found the little old man waiting for him in the forest.

"I have not forgotten your kindness," he said. "Now look behind you." Then, with a great rustling of canvas, the most magnificent ship sailed into the glade.

When the King saw the ship sailing over the fields towards his palace he knew he would have to give in and so Dummling and the Princess were married.

They lived happily ever after but back at home Dummling's two brothers grew bitter and miserable — and all for the lack of a good, generous heart.

LAZY TEDDY

There was nothing Lazy Teddy liked more than to be tucked up snug and warm in Joshua's bed. Every morning the alarm clock would ring and Joshua would leap out of bed and fling open the curtains. "I love mornings!" he'd say, stretching his arms up high as the sun poured in through the window. "You're crazy!" Teddy would mutter, and he'd burrow down beneath the quilt to the bottom of the bed, where he'd spend the rest of the morning snoozing happily.

"Come out and play, you lazy bear," Joshua would call. But Lazy Teddy wouldn't budge. He would just snore even louder.

Joshua wished that Teddy would be more lively, like his other friends' bears. He loved having adventures, but they would be even better if Teddy would share them with him.

One evening, Joshua decided to have a talk with Teddy before they went to bed. He told him all about the fishing trip he'd been on that day with his friends and their teddy bears.

"It was lots of fun, Teddy. I wish you'd been there. It really is time you stopped being such a lazybones. Tomorrow is my birthday, and I'm having a party. There will be games, and presents and ice-cream. Please promise you'll come?"

"It does sound like fun," said Teddy. "Okay, I promise. I'll get up just this once."

The next morning, Joshua was up bright and early. "Yippee, it's my birthday today!" he yelled, dancing round the room. He pulled the covers off his bed. "Come on, Teddy, time to get up!"

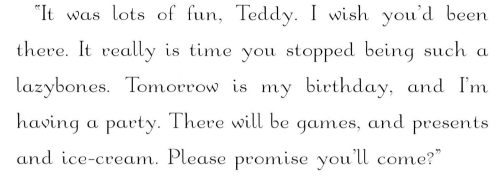

"Just five more minutes!" groaned Teddy, and he rolled over and fell straight back to sleep. When Joshua came back up to his room after breakfast, Teddy still wasn't up. Well, by now Joshua was getting quite cross with Teddy. He reached over and poked him in the tummy. Teddy opened one eye and growled. "Wake up, Teddy! You promised, remember?" said Joshua.

Teddy yawned. "Oh, if I must!" he said, and muttering and grumbling he climbed out of bed. He washed his face and paws, brushed his teeth and put on his best red vest.

"There, I'm ready!" he said.

"Good," said Joshua. "About time too!"

Just then the doorbell rang, and Joshua ran to answer it. "I'll come and fetch you in a minute," he said to Teddy. But when he returned there was no sign of Teddy, just a gentle snoring coming from the bottom of the bed.

Joshua was so cross and upset with Lazy Teddy, that he decided to leave him right where he was.

"He'll just have to miss the party!" he said. Deep down though, he was hurt that Teddy wouldn't keep his promise.

Joshua enjoyed his party, although he wished that Teddy had been there. That night when he got into bed, he lay crying quietly into his pillow.

Teddy lay awake in the dark, listening. He knew Joshua was crying because he had let him down, and he felt very ashamed of himself.

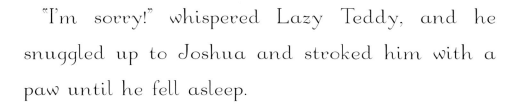

"I'm sorry!" whispered Lazy Teddy, and he snuggled up to Joshua and stroked him with a paw until he fell asleep.

The next morning when the alarm clock rang, Joshua leapt out of bed, as usual. But what was this? Teddy had leapt out of bed too, and was stretching his paws up high. Joshua looked at him in amazement.

"What are we doing today, then?" asked Teddy.

"G...g...going for a picnic," stammered Joshua, in surprise. "Are you coming?"

"Of course," said Teddy. And from that day on, Teddy was up bright and early every day, ready to enjoy another day of adventures with Joshua, and he never let him down again.

GEE UP, TEDDY

Gee up, Teddy,
Don't you stop!
Ride on the
hobbyhorse,
Clippety clop!
Clippety clopping,
Round and round.
Giddy up,
We're toybox bound!

THREE TEDS IN A TUB

Rub-a-dub, dub,
Three teds in a tub,
Sailing across the sea!
But the rumble of tums,
And the smell of hot buns,
Will bring them back home for tea!

LITTLE DOG LOST

"Brrr," shivered Scruffy. "It's cold tonight."

"Well, snuggle up closer to me," said his mom.

"It's not fair," Scruffy grumbled. "Why do we have to sleep outside in the cold? The cats are allowed to sleep inside, in nice warm baskets!"

"We're farm dogs, dear," said Mom. "We have to be tough, and work hard to earn our keep."

"I'd rather be a cat," mumbled Scruffy. "All they do is wash themselves, eat and sleep."

"We don't have such a bad life," said Mom. "Now stop feeling sorry for yourself, and get some rest. We've got a lot of work to do tomorrow."

The next day, Scruffy woke early and trotted down the lane for a walk. He ran through the grass, chasing rabbits, and sniffing at the flowers.

Now, usually when he got to the end of the lane he stopped and turned back. But today, he saw a big red truck parked outside a house there. The back of the truck was open, and Scruffy thought he would just climb inside and take a look.

The truck was full of furniture. At the back was a big armchair with soft cushions. Scruffy clambered onto it. "I could doze all day, like a cat!" he told himself. He closed his eyes and before he knew it he had fallen fast asleep.

Scruffy awoke some time later with a sharp jolt.

"Oh, no, I fell asleep!" he groaned. "I'd better hurry back. We've got a busy day ahead!"

But then he saw that the truck doors were closed! He could hear voices outside.

"Oh, dear, I'll be in trouble if I get found in here," thought Scruffy, and he hid behind the chair.

The back of the truck opened and Scruffy peered out. Two men started unloading the furniture.

When Scruffy was sure that no one was looking, he crept out of the truck, but he was no longer in the countryside where he lived! He was in a big noisy town, full of buildings and cars.

Poor Scruffy had no idea where he was!

"The truck must have carried me away," thought Scruffy, feeling frightened.

All day long, Scruffy roamed around trying to find his way home, feeling cold, tired and hungry. At last, he lay down and began to howl miserably.

"What's the matter, pup?" he heard a man's kind voice say. "You look lost. Come home with me." Scruffy gave the man's hand a grateful lick, then jumped up and followed him home.

When they arrived at the man's house Scruffy sat on the doorstep, hoping the man might bring him some food out to eat. But the man said, "Come on in, you can't stay out there."

Scruffy followed the man in, and found a little poodle waiting to meet him. Scruffy stared at her in amazement. What had happened to her fur?

"You'd better take a bath before supper," said the man, looking at Scruffy's dirty white coat. The man washed him in a big tub, then brushed his tangled coat. Scruffy howled miserably. What had he done to deserve such punishment?

"Don't you like it?" asked the poodle, shyly.

"No, I don't," said Scruffy. "All this washing and cleaning is for cats!"

Next the man gave them supper — small bowls of dry pellets. Scruffy sniffed at them in disgust. He was used to chunks of meat and a nice big bone.

"This looks like cat food," said Scruffy, miserably.

After supper the poodle climbed into a big basket in the kitchen.

"I thought that belonged to a cat," said Scruffy. He tried sleeping in the basket but he was hot and uncomfortable. He missed counting the stars to help him fall asleep, and most of all he missed his mom.

"I want to go home," he cried, and big tears slipped down his nose.

The next day, the man put Scruffy on a lead and took him into town. He hated being dragged along, without being able to sniff at things.

Then, as they crossed the market place, Scruffy heard a familiar bark, and saw his mom's head hanging through the window of the farmer's truck! He started to howl, dragged the man over to where the truck was parked, then leapt up at the window barking excitedly. The farmer could hardly believe it was Scruffy — he had never seen him so clean! The man explained how he had found Scruffy, and the farmer thanked the man for taking such good care of him.

On the way back home, Scruffy told his mom all about his adventure and what had happened.

"I thought you had run away because you didn't like being a farm dog," she said gently.

"Oh, no, Mom," said Scruffy, quickly. "I love being a farm dog. I can't wait to get home to a nice big juicy bone and our little bed beneath the stars!"

FIVE LITTLE DUCKLINGS

One, two, three, four, five,
Five little ducklings duck and dive,
Six, seven, eight, nine, ten,
Then swim home in a row again!

Why do they swim in rows?
The answer is nobody knows!
I wonder, as they swim past,
Who goes first and who goes last?

To the tune of 'Once I Caught A Fish Alive.'

CAT'S CHORUS

We meet every night
On the same garden wall,
And if you're in luck
You may hear our call:
*With howl and a yowl, and a hullaballoo,
We're the cat's chorus, singing for you!*

Fifi's soprano,
Butch sings the bass,
Kipper's a baritone,
Bert sets the pace.

Chorus

We sing lots of songs
Both new ones and old,
All huddled together
To keep out the cold.

Chorus

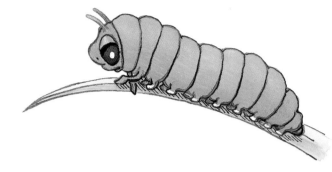

The Jealous Caterpillar

One spring day a green caterpillar sat on a leaf. He watched a beautiful butterfly flutter past him on the breeze. "It's not fair. Here I am stuck on this boring leaf with nothing to do and nowhere to go while that lucky creature can fly across the world and see far-off lands," thought the caterpillar crossly. "And what's more," he continued to himself, "not only has that butterfly got wings with which to fly, but he's beautiful, too. Look at poor me. I'm just a dull green. No-one will notice me because I'm the same color as the leaf." The caterpillar really did feel very sorry for himself, and rather jealous. "Go and enjoy yourself. Don't worry about me," he called spitefully to the butterfly.

But the butterfly hadn't heard a single word the caterpillar had been muttering, and soon he flew away. The caterpillar suddenly decided that he was going to be like the butterfly. "I'll learn how to fly and I'll paint myself lovely colors so that I look beautiful, too," he thought. He looked around for something to paint himself with but, of course, there was nothing at all on the leaf. Then he tried to fly. He launched himself from his leaf and tried to flap his tail, but all he did was land on the leaf below.

Along came a ladybug. "Aha!" thought the caterpillar. "Here's a beautiful creature who knows how to fly. I'll ask her to teach me." So the caterpillar said, "Hello, I've been admiring your beautiful wingcase. Could you tell me how I, too, could be beautiful? And can you teach me to fly?"

The ladybug looked at the caterpillar. "Be patient and wait a while," she said wisely, "and soon enough you'll get what you want." And with that the ladybug went on her way.

"Whatever can she mean? She's just too proud to teach me," the caterpillar thought jealously.

Some time later a bee buzzed past and landed on a nearby leaf. "Aha!" thought the caterpillar. "Here's a beautiful creature who knows how to fly. I'll ask him to teach me." So the caterpillar said, "Hello, I've been admiring your beautiful striped back. Could you tell me how I, too, could be beautiful? And can you teach me to fly?"

The bee looked at the caterpillar. "You'll find out soon enough, young man," said the bee sternly. And with that he went on his way.

"Whatever can he mean? He's just too haughty to teach me," the caterpillar thought jealously.

Now a while later along came a bird. "Aha!" thought the caterpillar once more. "Here's a beautiful creature who knows how to fly. I'll ask him to teach me." So once again the caterpillar said, "Hello, I've been admiring your beautiful feathers. Could you tell me how I, too, could be beautiful? And can you teach me to fly?"

The bird looked at the caterpillar and thought to himself slyly that here was a very silly caterpillar, but he would make a tasty snack for his chicks. "Let's see if I can trick him," he thought.

"I can't give you wings and I can't make you beautiful. But I can show you the world. I expect you'd like to see the world, wouldn't you, little caterpillar?" said the bird.

"Oh, yes!" said the caterpillar in great excitement.

"Climb upon my back then, little caterpillar!" said the crafty bird.

The caterpillar did as he was told and the bird flew off towards his nest. At first the caterpillar clung tightly to the bird's back but soon he felt quite sleepy and eventually he dozed off and slipped from the bird's back. Down he fell through the air and landed on a leaf, but still he didn't wake up. Soon he was wrapped in a soft, brown, papery cocoon from which he would not wake up for a long while.

Meanwhile, the bird reached his nest. "Look at the treat I've brought you," he said to his chicks.

They looked very puzzled. "What treat, Dad?" one of them piped up.

"This nice juicy caterpillar," said the bird, shaking the feathers on his back. "Climb down, little caterpillar," he said. But of course there was nothing there. Now it was the father's turn to look puzzled, while the chicks laughed at him.

"Well, I must have dropped him," he said. "I've never done that before," he added. He flew out of the nest in search of the caterpillar but he was nowhere to be seen. Once he saw a strange brown, papery parcel on a leaf, but in the end the bird had to return to the nest with his beak empty.

A long while later the caterpillar woke up. "I must get out of this stuffy wrapping," he thought, as he pushed his way out. He stood on the leaf and yawned and stretched. As he stretched, he noticed to his amazement two pairs of beautiful wings spreading out on either side of his body. "Are they really mine?" he wondered. He tried lifting and turning them and yes, he could make them work. He looked at his reflection in a raindrop and saw a lovely butterfly staring back at him.

"So the ladybug and the bee were right," he exclaimed. "How foolish I was to be a jealous caterpillar," he declared to a passing ant, "for now I am a beautiful butterfly after all."

The Greedy Hamster

There was once a hamster named Harry. He was a very greedy hamster. As soon as his food was put in his cage he gobbled it all up, and then he would push his little nose through the bars in the hope that something else to eat might come within reach. From his cage he could see all manner of delicious food on the kitchen table – and the smells! The scent of freshly baked bread was enough to send him spinning round in his exercise wheel with frustration.

"It's not fair!" he grumbled to himself. "They're all eating themselves silly out there and here I am simply starving to death!" (At this point he would usually remember the large meal he had just eaten and that his tummy was indeed still rather full.)

"If only I could get out of this rotten cage, I could feast on all the food I deserve," he announced to himself, and the thought of all those tasty morsels made his mouth water.

One night after the family had gone to bed, Harry was having one last spin in his wheel before retiring to his sawdust mattress. As he spun around, he heard an unfamiliar squeaky noise.

"That's funny," thought Harry. "The little girl oiled my wheel only today. It surely can't need oiling again." He stopped running and got off the wheel, but the squeak continued. Harry sat quite still on his haunches and listened intently. Then he realized it was the door to his cage squeaking. The door! The door was flapping open. The little girl had not closed it properly before she went to bed. Harry did a little dance of glee. Then he went to the door and looked cautiously out in case there was any danger. But all seemed to be well. The cat was asleep on a chair. The dog was sleeping soundly on the floor.

Now, as well as being a greedy hamster, Harry was also clever. Once outside the cage, the first thing he did was look at the catch to see how it worked. Yes! He was pretty sure he could work out how to open it from the inside now. Harry sniffed the air. There were some tasty titbits left over from a birthday party on the table. He could smell the sugar icing, and soon he was on the table, cramming his mouth with odds and ends of cheese sandwiches and pieces of chocolate cake. When he had eaten his fill, he stuffed his cheek pouches with ginger cookies and ran back into his cage, closing the door behind him.

"Good!" thought Harry. "Now I will never be hungry again."

The next night Harry let himself out of his cage and helped himself to food, and again the next night and the night after that. He feasted on everything and anything – nuts, bananas, pieces of bread, left-over jello and slices of pizza were all pushed into his greedy mouth. Each time he returned to his cage he filled his cheeks with more and more food. He did not notice that he was getting fatter and fatter, although he was aware that he could no longer run round in his wheel without falling off! Then one night, he undid the door catch but found he was simply too wide to get through the door!

For a while Harry sat in a very bad temper in the corner of the cage. His cheeks were still bulging with food from his last midnight feast, but the greedy hamster wanted more. Then he had an idea. "I'll get that lazy cat to help," he thought. He squealed at the top of his voice until the cat, who had been dreaming of rats, woke up with a start.

"What do you want?" she hissed at Harry. Harry explained his problem.

"Of course, I'd be only too pleased to help," said the crafty cat, thinking to herself here was an extra dinner! With her strong claws she bent back the door frame of the cage, until there was just enough room for Harry to squeeze through. Then, with a mighty swipe of her paw, she caught him and gobbled him whole. She felt extremely full, what with Harry and all his food inside her. She could barely crawl back to her chair and soon she was fast asleep again and snoring loudly with her mouth open. Inside her tummy Harry, too, felt very uncomfortable. Every time the cat snored, it sounded like a thunderstorm raging around his head.

"I must get out of here," he thought, and headed for the cat's open jaws. But he was far too fat to get out again. Then he had another idea. Through the cat's jaws he could see the dog lying on the floor.

"Help! Help!" he squeaked. The dog woke up to a very strange sight. There was the cat lying on the chair snoring, but she also seemed to be squeaking, "Help!" The dog put his head on one side. He was very perplexed. Then he saw a pair of beady eyes and some fine whiskers inside the cat's mouth. It was Harry!

"Get me out of here, please," pleaded Harry.

Now the dog did not very much like the cat, so he was quite willing to help the hamster.

"I'll stick my tail in the cat's mouth. Then you hang on while I pull you out," said the dog. "But mind you don't make a sound and wake the cat, or she'll surely bite my tail!" The dog gingerly put the tip of his tail inside the cat's open jaws, just far enough for Harry's little paws to grab hold. Then he pulled with all his might. Out popped Harry and out of Harry popped all the food he'd stored in his cheeks – peanuts, an apple core and a slice of jam tart!

"Thank you, thank you," gasped Harry as he made a dash for his cage and slammed the door shut. "I think I'll stay in my cage from now on and just stick to the food I'm given!"

Rapunzel

There once lived a man and his wife who had long wished for a child. At last their wish was granted and the wife found that she was expecting a baby. At the back of their house was a garden that was filled with the most beautiful flowers and herbs. However, the man and his wife did not dare enter the garden, for it was owned by a wicked witch, of whom everyone was scared.

One day, when the woman was standing by her window looking down into the garden, she saw a flower bed full of the prettiest Rapunzel plants she had ever seen. They looked so fresh and green that she felt a great craving to eat some of them. Day after day she would sit by her window, staring at the Rapunzel plants for hours on end. Eventually she became quite pale and miserable..

"What's wrong, my dear?" said her husband.

"I must have some of that Rapunzel," she replied, "or I may die."

The poor husband decided that the only thing to do was to steal into the witch's garden at night and take some of the plants. Late one night the man climbed the high wall that surrounded the garden and hastily snatched a bunch of Rapunzel plants and made off with them.

His wife was delighted. She made a salad of them that was so delicious that the next day she said to her husband, "I must have more of that delicious Rapunzel."

So that night the husband stole once more into the witch's garden. Imagine his horror when he dropped on to the grass to find the witch there lying in wait for him. "How dare you come into my garden and steal my Rapunzel plants," she shrieked. "You'll live to regret this."

"Please have mercy on me," begged the man. "I'm not really a thief. I came to help my wife, who is expecting our first child. She told me she would die if she didn't have some of your Rapunzel to eat."

Then the witch changed her tune. "By all means," she said, "take as much as you like. But in exchange you must give me the baby when it is born. Don't worry – I will care for it as if I were its mother. What do you say?" The man was so terrified that he hastily agreed to what the witch had said. When his wife gave birth to a baby girl the witch immediately appeared to take the child. The witch named her Rapunzel, after the plants that had caused all the trouble, and took the child away with her.

Rapunzel grew very beautiful, strong and healthy, with long golden hair that fell past her waist. When she was twelve years old the witch locked her away at the top of a tower in the middle of a forest. The tower had neither stairs nor a door, but only one window at the top so that nobody but the witch could reach her.

Each day when the witch visited her, she would stand below the girl's window and call out, "Rapunzel, Rapunzel, let down your hair, that I may climb without a stair."

Then the girl would wind her long tresses around the window hook and lower her hair all the way to the ground. The witch would climb up it as if it were a ladder. In this way, Rapunzel's lonely life went on for several years.

One day, a young prince was riding in the forest when he heard a sweet voice. It was Rapunzel singing to herself. The prince was so entranced that he followed the sound and came upon the tower.

But when he could find no way in he became discouraged and rode home. Rapunzel's lovely voice had stirred his heart so deeply, however, that he returned day after day to hear her singing.

One day, as he stood behind a tree, he saw the witch appear and heard her calling, "Rapunzel, Rapunzel, let down your hair, that I may climb without a stair."

Then he saw a mass of golden hair tumble down and watched the witch climb up it to the window. "Is that the way up?" thought the prince. "Then I will climb the golden ladder, too."

The next day, around dusk, the prince went to the tower and called, "Rapunzel, Rapunzel, let down your hair, that I may climb without a stair."

Immediately the tresses fell down and the prince climbed up. At first sight of the prince, Rapunzel was afraid, but the prince addressed her in such a friendly way that she knew she could trust him. "Once I had heard your voice," said the prince, "I couldn't rest until I saw you. Now I cannot rest until you agree to marry me."

Rapunzel by now had fallen truly in love with the young man, so she willingly accepted. "I wish I could come away with you," said Rapunzel. "You must bring some silk with you each time you visit, and I shall weave a ladder of silk and then I will be able to escape."

Each day the witch visited Rapunzel and each night the prince came. The witch suspected nothing until one day Rapunzel forgot herself and said to the witch, "Why are you so much heavier to pull up than the prince?"

"Oh, treacherous girl," screamed the witch. "You have deceived me!" She snatched up a pair of scissors and cut off all Rapunzel's lovely hair. Then the witch drove Rapunzel from the tower and left her in a wild and desolate place to fend for herself as best she could.

That night, along came the prince to the tower and said, as usual, "Rapunzel, Rapunzel, let down your hair, that I may climb without a stair."

But the witch was lying in wait. She tied Rapunzel's hair to the window hook and let the golden tresses fall to the ground. Up climbed the prince full of joy, as always. But when he stepped in through the window, it was not his beautiful Rapunzel that met his gaze but the icy glare of the witch. "Aha!" cried the witch with a sneer. "So you thought you could steal my girl, did you? Well she's gone and you'll never set eyes on her again."

Beside himself with grief, the prince threw himself from the tower and would have died had he not landed in the thickest briars. Although he survived, the thorns pierced his eyes and blinded him. For many years he wandered through the wilderness grieving for his lost Rapunzel and living on whatever he could find to eat. Eventually, he wandered into the same part of the wilderness where Rapunzel lived in miserable poverty with the twins she had borne.

Just as he had done so many years ago, the prince heard a sweet voice coming through the trees. He made his way towards the sound of the voice. Suddenly Rapunzel saw him and straight away she recognised him. She ran to him and threw her arms around him weeping. As she wept tears of joy and sorrow, two teardrops fell into his eyes, healing them and restoring his sight.

Then the two were united again and the prince took Rapunzel and their children back to his own kingdom, and they all lived happily ever after.

As Small as a Mouse

As small as a mouse,

As wide as a bridge,

As tall as a house,

As straight as a pin.

154

Slowly, Slowly

Slowly, slowly, very slowly
Creeps the garden snail.

Slowly, slowly, very slowly
Up the garden rail.

Quickly, quickly, very quickly
Runs the little mouse.

Quickly, quickly, very quickly
Round about the house.

Walk hand slowly up baby's tummy...

Tickle baby during second verse

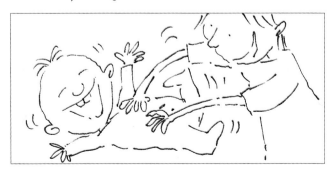

Row, Row, Row Your Boat

Row, row, row your boat,
Gently down the stream,
Merrily, merrily, merrily, merrily,
Life is but a dream.

Mime rowing action throughout...

Round About There

Round about there,
Sat a little hare,
A cat came and
chased him,
Right up there!

Circle child's palm with finger

ROUND ABOUT THERE

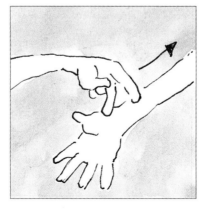

Walk fingers up arm

A CAT CAME AND CHASED HIM

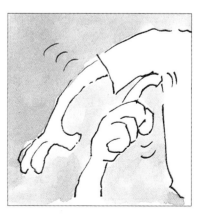

Tickle!

RIGHT UP THERE!

One Man Went To Mow

One man went to mow, went to mow a meadow,
One man and his dog, Spot,
Went to mow a meadow.

Two men went to mow, went to mow a meadow,
Two men, one man and his dog, Spot,
Went to mow a meadow.

Three men went to mow, went to mow a meadow,

Three men, two men, one man and his dog, Spot,

Went to mow a meadow.

Four men went to mow, went to mow a meadow,

Four men, three men, two men, one man and his dog, Spot,

Went to mow a meadow.

Five men went to mow, went to mow a meadow,

Five men, four men, three men, two men,

one man and his dog, Spot,

Went to mow a meadow.

The Grand Old Duke of York

The grand old Duke of York,

He had ten thousand men;

He marched them up to the top of the hill;

Then he marched them down again.

And when they were up they were up.

And when they were down they were down.

And when they were only halfway up,

They were neither up nor down.

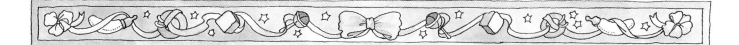

Bye, Baby Bunting

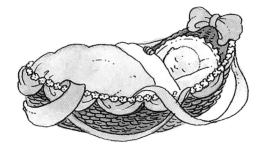

Bye, Baby Bunting

Daddy's gone a-hunting,

To find a little rabbit skin,

To wrap his Baby Bunting in.

Ursula's Umbrella

Ursula was a little girl who longed for adventure. She loved reading stories about far-away places and explorers, and even children like herself who had amazing adventures. "Why doesn't anything interesting ever happen to me?" she sighed. "How I wish I could fly to the moon or dive to the deepest part of the ocean. What fun it would be!"

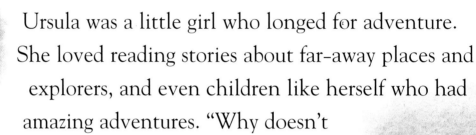

One windy day, Ursula went out for a walk. She took her umbrella with her because it looked as though it might be going to rain. Ursula's umbrella was red with a shiny black handle. It was also very large indeed. People used to laugh as Ursula walked along the street with her umbrella up. It looked so big and Ursula was so small that it seemed as though the umbrella was walking along all by itself!

As Ursula walked up the street she felt a few raindrops on her nose. "Better put up my umbrella," she thought. She unfurled her umbrella and lifted it up above her head. As she did so, a great gust of wind came and swept her right off the pavement. It carried her past the upstairs windows of the houses, past the roofs and the chimney pots and up, up, into the sky. Ursula clung tightly to the umbrella handle. She was surprised to find she didn't feel the least bit frightened. No, not a bit. She felt very excited. She looked down and saw streets and houses whizzing past far below. Then she saw fields and something that looked like a silver thread snaking through the countryside. "A river!" thought Ursula.

Now she could see the coastline, and soon the umbrella was carrying her out over the ocean. At first when she looked down the sea was gray, but gradually it turned to the deepest blue with frothy white waves. "How I'd love a swim," thought Ursula. At that moment she felt the umbrella starting to descend. Looking down she could see that they were heading for an island in the middle of the ocean. Soon she was floating past the tops of palm trees and, as she touched the ground, she felt sand under her feet.

"I'm going for a swim!" said Ursula to herself. She folded up her umbrella and set off to the beach. The water felt deliciously warm as Ursula paddled about. She looked down and saw that the water was amazingly clear. She could see brightly colored fish darting in and out of the coral. "Wow!" exclaimed Ursula out loud and then "Wow!" again, though this time much louder as she looked up and saw a black fin skimming through the water towards her. "Shark!" she shrieked, but no-one heard.

Then all of a sudden a gust of wind made her umbrella unfurl itself and float towards her in the water, like a boat. Ursula made a dash for the umbrella, hurled herself into it and floated away across the sea. "That was quite an adventure!" she thought.

164

After a while, Ursula looked out over the rim of the umbrella and saw that it was heading for the shore again. This time, when Ursula stepped out of the umbrella, she found that she was at the edge of a jungle. Folding up the umbrella, she set off into the forest. She followed an overgrown path through the trees. "I wonder where this leads?" thought Ursula. She wiped her brow and swatted the insects that flew in front of her face. Deeper and deeper into the jungle she went.

Suddenly she heard the sound of rushing water and found herself standing on the banks of a river. All at once she heard another sound. It was the crashing noise of some enormous beast approaching through the trees.

Where could she run to? Suddenly she felt the umbrella being blown from her hand. To her amazement it fell to the ground, stretching right across the river like a bridge. Ursula walked over to the other side, not daring to look down at the torrent below. When she was safely on the far bank she looked back to see a large puma, with glittering green eyes, glaring at her from the opposite bank. "That was a lucky escape!" thought Ursula.

Ursula could see a mountain through the trees and decided to head towards it. "I'll be able to get a good view from the top and maybe find my way home," she thought. She struggled on through the forest and eventually found herself at the foot of the mountain. There seemed to be no way up the sheer rock face. Ursula was on the point of despair when suddenly another great gust of wind blew up. It carried Ursula, clinging to her opened umbrella, all the way up to the top of the mountain.

At the top of the mountain, the umbrella let her gently down again and her feet landed in deep snow. By now it was blowing a blizzard and she could not see anything except white snowflakes in all directions. "There's only one thing to do," thought Ursula. She put the umbrella on the snow, sat on it and whizzed all the way down the other side of the mountain.

When she reached the bottom, to her surprise, the umbrella sled didn't stop but carried on through the snowstorm until eventually, after a very long time, it came to a halt right outside her own front door. "Well, that was quite an adventure," said Ursula, shaking the snow off the umbrella, before folding it up.

She stepped inside the front door. "Wherever have you been?" said her mother. "You look as though you've been to the ends of the Earth and back."

"Well I have," Ursula was about to say. But then she thought that no-one would believe her and it was nicer to keep her adventures to herself. And that is what she did.

The Dragon Who Was Scared of Flying

Once upon a time, in a land far away, there lived a dragon named Dennis. He lived in a cave high up in the mountains. All his friends lived in caves nearby, and his own brothers and sisters lived right next door. Now you would think that Dennis would have been a very happy dragon, surrounded by his friends and family, wouldn't you? Well, I'm sorry to say that Dennis was, in fact, a very unhappy and lonely dragon.

The reason for this was that Dennis was scared of flying. Every day his friends would set off to have adventures, leaving poor Dennis behind on his own. Dennis would stare out of his cave at the departing dragons. How he wished he could join them!

After they had gone, he would stand on the ledge outside his cave, trying to build up the courage to fly. But as soon as he looked over the edge, he felt all giddy and had to step back. Then he would crawl back into his cave defeated and spend the rest of the day counting stalagtites on the ceiling or rearranging his collection of bat bones.

Every evening, the other dragons would return with amazing tales of what they had been up to that day. "I rescued a damsel in distress," one would say.

"I fought the wicked one-eyed giant and won," boasted another.

"I helped light the fire for a witch's cauldron," announced a third.

"What have you been up to?" Dennis's sister Doreen used to ask him.

"Oh... um... this and that," Dennis would reply mournfully, looking down at his scaly toes. Then Doreen would lead him out of the cave and try to teach him to fly. Dennis would take a running jump and flap his wings furiously but his feet would stay firmly on the ground. Then the other dragons would laugh so much that, in the end, he always gave up.

One day, Dennis could stand it no longer. The other dragons flew off as usual to find adventure but Dennis, instead of retreating into his cave, set off down the mountain side. It was very tiring having to walk. Dennis had never really been further than from his cave to the ledge and back, and soon he was puffing and panting. He was about to rest at the side of the path when his eye was caught by something colorful in the distance. Down in the valley he could make out some brightly colored tents, and now he could hear the faint strains of music drifting up to him. "I'd better take a closer look," thought Dennis. "Maybe I can have an adventure, like the other dragons!" He got so excited at the thought of his very own adventure that he started to run. Then he got all out of breath and had to stop altogether for a while.

At last Dennis reached the tents and found himself in a world more exotic than he could ever have imagined. He was surrounded by strange, four-legged creatures, such as he had never seen before. There was a yellow creature that roared and another one with stripes and fierce teeth. There were also quite a few hairy creatures with long tails. These ones were dressed up to look like boys and girls. Can you guess what all these creatures were? Of course, Dennis had never seen a lion or a tiger or a chimpanzee before. He thought they were very peculiar! The animals thought Dennis was very odd, too. They stood in a circle around him. "How strange," snarled the lion. "A slimy thing with wings!"

"It doesn't look very fit!" growled the tiger, flexing his claws.

"Look at its funny, knobbly tail," giggled the chimpanzees.

Dennis began to feel unhappy and unwanted again, but at that moment he heard a friendly voice saying, "Hello, there! Welcome to Chippy's Circus. I'm Claude the clown. How do you do?"

Dennis turned round. Now he felt really confused, for standing behind him was a man with the unhappiest face Dennis had ever seen. He had great sad eyes and a mouth that was turned down so far that it seemed to touch his chin. Yet he spoke so cheerfully!

"I'm Dennis the dragon," said Dennis.

"A dragon, eh?" said Claude. "Well, we've never had a dragon in the circus before. Might be quite a crowd puller! Would you like to join the circus?" he asked.

"Oh, yes please," cried Dennis.

"Very well," said Claude. "I'm sure you're very talented," he added.

So Dennis joined the circus and was happy for the first time in his life. The other animals became quite friendly now that they knew what he was. Claude taught Dennis to ride the unicycle and to do acrobatic tricks. He also learned how to dive into a bucket of water. He didn't mind that a bit because his slimy skin was quite waterproof! Now, as you know, dragons are particularly

172

good at breathing fire, so Dennis soon became the circus's champion fire-eater. Folk would come from far and near to see Dennis shooting flames high into the dark roof of the big top.

One evening Dennis had just finished his fire-eating act. He was eating an icecream to cool his hot throat and watching Carlotta, the tight-rope walker. She was pirouetting high up on the rope as usual. Then all at once she lost her footing and Dennis saw to his horror that she was going to fall. He dropped his icecream and, without thinking, flapped his wings furiously. As Carlotta fell, Dennis found himself flying up towards her. He caught her gently on his back and flew down to the ground with her clinging on tightly. The crowd roared and burst into applause. They obviously thought it was all part of the act.

"Thank you, Dennis," whispered Carlotta in Dennis's ear. "You saved my life."

Dennis was overjoyed. Not only had he saved Carlotta's life, he had also learned to fly. And he said with a grin, "I do declare that flying is actually rather fun."

The Ugly Duckling

There was once a little mother duck. She had six eggs in her nest and there she sat day after day in the summer sun patiently waiting for them to hatch. Five of the eggs were small and white but the sixth egg was large and brown. The little duck often wondered why that egg was so different.

One morning she heard a crack, then another, then another. Her chicks were ready! One by one they tumbled from their shells and soon five little chicks were gathered under the wings of their proud mother. But the large brown egg had not hatched.

"What can be keeping my last little chick?" thought the mother duck to herself and she settled herself on top of the egg to keep it warm.

At last she felt the egg moving and out scrambled a chick. But this chick was nothing like her other babies. He was covered in dull brown fluff and had a long scrawny neck. He wasn't nearly as pretty as his brothers and sisters. But the mother duck loved him just the same and took care to protect him from the other farmyard animals who often teased him.

"Did you ever see anything quite as ugly as that gawky looking creature?" squawked a large brown duck to his friend, the white hen.

"Go away!" clucked the hen. "We don't want you in our farmyard," and she pecked at the poor little duckling with her sharp beak.

Not a day passed by without one animal or another making fun of the duckling so at last he decided he would run away. One dark night he crept away quietly while everyone was asleep and headed for the open fields. By daybreak he was quite exhausted.

"I will rest for a while," he said to himself and was soon fast asleep. But he awoke just two minutes later to feel the hot breath of a large animal wafting over him. Peeking out from under his wing he was terrified to see a fierce beast with a long red tongue! It was a hunting dog but to the duckling's great relief it simply sniffed him and then padded away across the moor.

"I am too ugly even for that dog to eat!" thought the duckling to himself sadly and he waddled off in search of somewhere to live. Not far away there was a cottage and for a time the duckling stayed there with an old lady, her hen and her cat. But they were not like him and as the days passed he longed to find some water so that he could splash about and swim.

"I must find a pond," he told the cat as he waved them goodbye. The weather grew colder and the snow began to fall. Suddenly the duckling heard a strange sound high above him and looking into the sky he saw a flock of white geese flying south for the winter

The duckling watched them go, spellbound. He had never seen anything so beautiful in all his life.

"If only I could go with them!" he sighed, "but what would those lovely creatures want with an ugly companion like me."

On he trudged and at last he reached a little pond — but how wretched he was when he saw that the water had turned to ice! There was one small patch of freezing water and there he splashed for a while but the cold had sapped his strength. Soon he found he could not get out of the water and back onto the land. After a while the ice crept closer and closer and then he was trapped. The duckling would surely have died if a man had not happened to pass by at that very moment. He saw the little creature stuck fast in the ice and took him home and warmed him in front of the fire. So the duckling spent the next few weeks being cared for by the kind man and his wife.

Soon the weather grew warmer and the duckling longed to be on his way once again.

"I must find a proper home for myself," he explained to the man and his wife as he waddled away.

The air grew softer, the birds sang and the flowers bloomed in the meadows once again. The duckling felt stronger and he noticed that his feet and his body had grown much bigger and seemed to be changing color. He felt happy and excited and, stretching out his wings, he beat them up and down for fun. Just imagine his astonishment when he suddenly found himself leaving the ground and flying through the air! What a glorious feeling it was to be soaring on high.

"Here in the sky I am free!" he said to himself happily. All at once he saw something exciting far below him. As he swooped down to get a better look he recognised the snow white birds who had flown over him on their way south. Now they had returned and were splashing in the pond. The duckling landed on the water and slowly swam towards them.

"I know I am ugly," he said shyly, "but please let me stay with you and be your friend."

"Why, you are not ugly!" laughed the birds. "You have become a beautiful swan just like us," and as the duckling bowed his head to look in the water he saw that it was indeed true!

JACK AND THE BEANSTALK

Once upon a time there lived a poor widow woman and her son Jack. He was a lazy boy and he would not tend the crops in the field. Soon the plants died and then they had no food to eat.

"All we have left to sell is our cow," said Jack's mother, and so the next day Jack set off down the road to the market. After a while he met a pedlar.

"I will buy your cow," offered the pedlar, "and in return I will give you these special beans," and he held out his hand. Jack inspected the six speckled beans.

"It's a deal," said Jack and he hurried back home again.

But when he showed his mother what he had been paid for the cow she was very angry! She boxed his ears and threw the beans straight out of the window.

"We cannot live on a handful of beans!" she cried, and they went to bed that night very hungry indeed. But when Jack awoke the next morning the first thing he saw when he opened his eyes were huge green leaves dangling outside his bedroom window.

"Look, mother!" he shouted. "The beans have taken root and grown into an enormous plant." Indeed the beanstalk was so tall that it towered high into the sky.

"I am going to climb up and see where the stalk ends," decided Jack. Soon he was as high as the roof.

"Come back! Come back!" called his mother, but Jack kept on climbing higher and higher and after a while the house was just a tiny spot far below him. Up and up Jack went and just when he felt his arms would drop he found himself stepping off the very last branch and onto firm ground. Nearby there stood a fine castle.

"Maybe I can get some food," thought the hungry boy. But when he knocked on the door he did not get a friendly welcome from the large lady who lived there.

"Go away!" she cried. "My husband is a fierce giant and he is particularly partial to small boys such as you." But Jack was so hungry that he begged to be allowed in, and at last the woman relented. Soon Jack found himself sitting at a huge kitchen table, happily nibbling a large piece of cheese. Suddenly the table shook and a loud roar filled the air.

"Fee, fi, fo, fum, I smell the blood of an Englishman!
Be he alive or be he dead,
I'll grind his bones to make my bread!"

"Quick, quick!" whispered the terrified woman. "You must hide for my husband is coming!" Hurriedly she bundled him into the oven and there Jack sat trembling like a leaf as the enormous giant strode into the kitchen and sniffed suspiciously.

"Hush, my dear. Don't fret! It is only the smell of your breakfast!" said his wife anxiously. "Come, sit and eat your food." Jack kept as quiet as a mouse as the giant shovelled the fried egg and bacon into his mouth.

"Now bring me my hen!" shouted the ogre.

The woman quickly fetched a small brown hen and placed it upon the table in front of him.

"Lay!" ordered the giant and to Jack's great astonishment the hen clucked loudly and instantly laid an egg. But this was no ordinary egg. No, this was a *golden* egg! The giant stroked the brown hen and smiled greedily. Then he yawned loudly, laid his great head upon his arms, and was soon fast asleep.

Jack was out of the oven and across the floor in a moment. Pausing only to grab the hen, he raced from the kitchen and out of the huge castle door. He ran for the beanstalk as fast as his legs could carry him and in no time at all he was back home with the hen still tucked tightly beneath his arm.

"Look, mother!" he cried. "This hen will lay as many golden eggs as we wish. We need never go hungry again."

But after a time Jack grew eager for adventure and decided to climb the beanstalk once more. The next day he dressed in a disguise and was soon up the beanstalk and knocking on the castle door.

The giant's wife looked at him suspiciously. "I foolishly admitted a small boy like you some months ago," she said, "and the ungrateful youth made off with my husband's favorite hen. I dare not risk letting you in." But Jack would not give up and so, once again, he found himself sitting at the giant's table. But what was this?

"Fee, fi, fo fum, I smell the blood of an Englishman!" The ogre was coming! Quickly Jack ran and hid in the oven. He peeked out as the ogre gulped down his meal.

"Bring me my money bags!" cried the giant when he had finished eating. Slowly he counted pile after pile of glittering golden coins but after a while he began to yawn and soon he was fast asleep. Jack jumped out of his hiding place, heaved a large money bag over his shoulder and ran like the wind away from the castle.

His mother was very thankful to see him safe and sound and what fun they had that night as they counted their new riches over and over again.

But after a time Jack grew restless and longed to visit the castle once more. His poor mother begged him to stay but all in vain for the next day Jack dressed in a different disguise and climbed the beanstalk.

This time the ogre's wife was more scared than ever.

"Some months ago another young fellow tricked me," she said. "He made off with my husband's money bag and oh! the trouble that caused me! The giant has been in a foul temper ever since."

But stubborn Jack would not be dissuaded and his fresh face looked so innocent that at last the poor woman gave in. But this time when Jack heard the giant's heavy footsteps thundering down the hall the oven was full of hot food and the only place that he could find to hide was inside the large washtub, surrounded by soapy socks.

The giant was indeed in a bad temper and he snarled and sniffed as he snooped around the kitchen. Under the bubbles, Jack shivered and kept as still as could be.

"What have we here?" the giant roared as he spotted the washtub. His wife wrung her hands nervously.

"Why, I am just washing your socks, dear," she said.

Luckily for Jack all giants hate water and with a grunt, the ogre turned aside and began to eat his meal.

"Bring me my harp!" he called to his wife as he threw down his last gnawed bone. In she hurried with a beautiful golden harp and it played the sweetest music Jack had ever heard. Soon the ogre was fast asleep and in a trice Jack leapt from the tub. He snatched up the harp and ran from the room but what a shock he got when the harp called out, "Master! Master!" With a cry of rage the ogre awoke and stumbled after little Jack. Out of the castle and down the beanstalk the terrified boy ran, with the giant close behind him all the way.

"Quick, mother, fetch the axe!" Jack shouted as he neared the ground. He swung the huge blade high in the air and with one mighty blow felled the plant. The giant gave a loud shriek, then tumbled from its branches and landed headfirst on the ground, stone dead.

And from that time on Jack and his mother enjoyed good luck and great happiness and Jack, having climbed the Ladder of Fortune and discovered that he had courage and an eager mind, was idle no more.

WOBBLY BEAR

Mr and Mrs Puppety owned an old-fashioned toy shop. They made toys by hand in a room at the back of the shop. But they were getting old and their eyesight was bad.

"It's time we got an apprentice toymaker," said Mr Puppety to his wife. They soon found a young lad called Tom to work for them. He worked hard and carefully. He spent his first week making a teddy bear. When he had finished he showed the bear to Mr and Mrs Puppety.

"He looks very cuddly," said Mrs Puppety.

Tom was pleased that they liked his bear and he went off home whistling happily.

"He is a lovely bear," said Mr Puppety, "but his head is a bit wobbly."

"I know," said his wife, "but it's Tom's first try. Let's just put him up there on the shelf with the other teddy bears."

That night Wobbly Bear sat on the shelf and started to cry. He had heard what Mr and Mrs Puppety had said about him.

"What's wrong?" asked Brown Bear, who was sitting next to him.

"My head is on wobbly," sobbed Wobbly Bear.

"Does it hurt?" asked Brown Bear.

"No," replied Wobbly Bear.

"Then why are you crying?" asked Brown Bear.

"Because nobody will want to buy a wobbly bear. I'll be left in this shop forever and nobody will ever take me home and love me," he cried.

"Don't worry," said Brown Bear. "We've all got our faults, and you look fine to me. Just try your best to look cute and cuddly and you'll soon have someone to love you." This made Wobbly Bear feel much happier and he soon fell fast asleep.

The next day the shop was full of people, but nobody paid any attention to Wobbly Bear. Then a little boy looked up at the shelf and cried, "Oh, what a lovely bear. Can I have that one, Daddy?"

Wobbly Bear's heart lifted as the little boy's daddy reached up to his shelf. But he picked up Brown Bear instead and handed him to the little boy. Wobbly Bear felt sadder than ever. Nobody wanted him. All of his new friends would get sold and leave the shop, but he would be left on the shelf gathering dust. Poor old Wobbly Bear!

Now, Mr and Mrs Puppety had a little grand-daughter called Jessie who loved to visit the shop and play with the toys. All the toys loved her because she was gentle and kind. It so happened that the next time she came to visit it was her birthday, and her grandparents told her she could choose any toy she wanted as her present.

"I know she won't choose me," thought Wobbly Bear sadly. "Not with all these other beautiful toys to choose from."

But to Wobbly's amazement, Jessie looked up and pointed at his shelf and said, "I'd like that wobbly bear please. No one else will have a bear quite like him."

Mr Puppety smiled and gave Wobbly to Jessie. She hugged and kissed him, and Wobbly felt so happy he almost cried. She took him home and put a smart red bow around his neck ready for her birthday party. He felt very proud indeed.

Soon the other children arrived, each carrying their teddy bears under their arms.

Wobbly Bear could not believe his eyes when he saw the little boy with his friend Brown Bear!

"I'm having a teddy bears' picnic," Jessie explained to him, hugging him tight. All of the children and the bears had a wonderful time, especially Wobbly. He had found a lovely home, met his old friend and made lots of new ones.

"See, I told you not to worry," said Brown Bear.

"I know," said Wobbly. "And I never will again."

TEDDY BEAR'S PICNIC

Little Bear brought chocolate cake,
Raggy Bear brought honey,
Baby Bear brought ice-cream,
With butterscotch all runny!

Tough Old Ted brought cinnamon-buns,
Silky Bear brought jello,
Shaggy Bear brought cookies and
Egg sandwiches all yellow!

Woolly Bear brought pecan pie,
Tiny Ted brought candy,
Mrs Bear brought little plates,
She thought would come in handy.

Off they set into the woods,
A sunny spot they found,
And had a teddies picnic,
As they shared the goodies round!

CROCODILE SMILES

"Say cheese!" said the photographer.

"CHEESE!" grinned Snappy, the crocodile. Lights flashed, and cameras clicked as he gave his most winning smile.

"You're a natural!" cried the expedition leader. He was with a team of wildlife photographers. Snappy smiled at his reflection in the river.

"Ooh, you are a handsome chap!" he preened, gnashing his fine set of teeth together with glee.

Snappy was terribly proud of his sharp fangs, and fine good looks. He strutted up and down the river bank for all to see.

"I'm a star!" he said. "My face will be known throughout the world!"

"Thanks for letting us take your picture," said the expedition leader.

"No problem," said Snappy. "Anytime!"

"And as your reward, here's the truckload of chocolate you asked for," said the leader.

"How delicious!" said Snappy. "Most kind of you. Thank you so much."

When they had gone, Snappy lay sunning himself on the river bank, daydreaming of fame and fortune, and popping chocolate after chocolate into his big, open mouth.

Just then, along slithered Snake.

"What's thissss?" he hissed. "A crocodile eating chocolate? How sssstrange!"

"Not at all!" snapped Snappy. "All crocodiles love chocolate. It's just that most of them aren't clever enough to know how to get hold of it."

"Well, if you're so sssmart, you ssshould know that too much chocolate will make your teeth fall out!" hissed Snake.

"What rot!" said Snappy, crossly. "For your information, I've got perfect teeth."

"Lucky you!" said Snake, and slithered off into the bushes.

So Snappy carried on munching happily, eating his way through the mound of chocolate. He had chocolate for breakfast, chocolate for lunch and chocolate for dinner.

"Ooh, yummy!" he grinned, licking his lips and smiling a big, chocolatey smile. "This is heaven."

"You won't be saying that when you are too fat to float in the river," said Parrot, who had been watching him from a tree.

"Nonsense!" scoffed Snappy. "I've got a very fine figure, I'll have you know!"

"If you say so," said Parrot, and flew off into the jungle.

Days and weeks passed, and Snappy happily carried on eating chocolate after chocolate, until at last it was all gone.

"Back to the river to catch my next meal, then," Snappy thought miserably. "Though I'd much rather have more chocolate!"

But when Snappy slid into the river, instead of bobbing gently at the surface, he sank straight to the bottom, and his stomach rested in the mud.

"Oh, dear, what's happened to the river?" Snappy wondered aloud to himself. "It's very hard to float in today."

"Even for someone with such a fine figure as you?" jeered Parrot, watching from the trees. Snappy didn't answer. He just sank further beneath the water so that only his two beady eyes could be seen, and gave Parrot a very hard stare.

The next morning when he awoke there was a terrible pain in his mouth. It felt like someone was twisting and tugging on his teeth. "Oww, my teeth hurt!" he cried.

"Sssurely not!" hissed Snake, dangling down from a tree. "After all, you have sssuch perfect teeth!" and he slunk away again, snickering.

Snappy knew what he had to do. He set off down the river to visit Mr Drill the dentist.

It seemed such a long hard walk, and by the time he got there he was puffing and panting.

"Open wide!" said Mr Drill, an anteater, peering down his long nose into Snappy's gaping mouth. "Oh, dear. This doesn't look good at all. What have you been eating, Snappy? Now show me where it hurts."

"Here," said Snappy pointing miserably into his mouth, and feeling rather ashamed, "and here, and here, and here..."

"Well, there's nothing for it," said Mr Drill, "they'll have to come out!" And so out they came!

Before long, another photography expedition arrived in the jungle.

"Say cheese!" said the expedition leader.

"CHEESE!" smiled Snappy, stepping out from behind a tree. But instead of a flash of cameras, Snappy met with howls of laughter, as the photographers fell about holding their sides.

"I thought you said Snappy was a handsome crocodile with perfect teeth!" they cried, looking at the leader. "He should be called Gappy, not Snappy!"

Poor Snappy slunk away into the bushes and cried. It was all his own fault for being so greedy and eating all that chocolate.

"There, there," said Mr Drill, patting his arm. "We'll soon fit you out with some fine new teeth."

And from then on, Snappy vowed he would never eat chocolate again!

ELEPHANTS NEVER FORGET

I woke up this morning, astounded,
To find my long trunk in a knot!
I know it must be to remind me
To remember something I've forgot!

But though I've been thinking all morning
I haven't remembered it yet.
Still I'm sure I will think of it soon,
Because elephants never forget!

ITCHY SPOTS

Poor Monkey was wriggling
And jiggling around,
Scratching and making
A chattering sound:

"They're driving me mad,
Someone help me please –
I have to get rid of
These terrible fleas!"

Then along came a bear
In a bit of a stew –
"I've got such a bad itch,
I don't know what to do!

It's right in a spot
I can't reach with my paws.
So why not scratch my back,
And I will scratch yours!"

The Lost Lion

Once there was a lion cub called Lenny. He was a very tiny lion cub, but he was sure that he was the bravest lion in all of Africa. When his mother taught her cubs how to stalk prey, Lenny would stalk his own mother and pounce on her. When she showed them how to wash themselves, Lenny licked his sister's face instead so that she growled at him. When the mother lioness led her cubs down to the watering hole to drink, he jumped into the water and created a huge splash that soaked everyone.

The other lionesses were not amused. "You'd better watch that son of yours," they said to Lenny's mother, "or he'll get into really big trouble."

One day the mother lioness led her
cubs on their first big hunt. "Stay close to me,"
she said, "or you could get hurt."
She crawled off through the undergrowth with
her cubs following on behind, one after the other. Lenny was at
the back. The grass tickled his tummy and he wanted to laugh,
but he was trying hard to be obedient. So he crawled along,
making sure he kept the bobbing tail of the cub in front in sight.
On and on they crawled until Lenny was beginning to feel
quite weary.

"But a brave lion cub doesn't give up," he thought to himself.
And on he plodded.

At last the grass gave way to a clearing. Lenny looked up, and to
his dismay he saw that the tail he had been following was attached,
not to one of his brothers or sisters, but to a baby elephant!

Somewhere along the trail he had started following the wrong tail and now he was hopelessly lost. He wanted to cry out for his mother but then he remembered that he was the bravest lion in all of Africa. So what do you think he did? He went straight up to the mother elephant and growled his fiercest growl at her. "That'll frighten her!" thought Lenny. "She won't dare growl back!" And, of course, she didn't growl back. Instead she lifted her trunk and trumpeted so loudly at Lenny that he was blown off his feet and through the air and landed against the hard trunk of a tree.

Lenny got up and found that his knees were knocking. "Oh my," he thought, "that elephant has a very loud growl. But I'm still definitely the bravest lion in all of Africa." He set off across the plain. It was getting hot in the midday sun and soon Lenny began to feel sleepy. "I think I'll just take a nap in that

tree," he thought, and started climbing up into the branches. To his surprise, he found that the tree was already occupied by a large leopard. "I'll show him who's boss," thought Lenny, baring his tiny claws. The leopard raised his head to look at Lenny, and then bared his own huge, razor-sharp claws. He took a swipe at Lenny with his paw. Without even touching Lenny, the wind from the leopard's great paw swept Lenny out of the tree and he landed with a bump on the ground.

Lenny got up and found that his legs were trembling. "Oh my," he thought, "that leopard had big claws. But I'm still definitely the bravest lion in Africa." He set off again across the plain. After a while he began to feel quite hungry. "I wonder what I can find to eat," he thought. Just then he saw a spotted shape lying low in the grass. "That looks like a tasty meal," thought Lenny as he pounced on the spotted shape

But the spotted shape was a cheetah! Quick as a flash, the cheetah sprang away and as he did so, his tail caught Lenny a blow that sent him spinning round and round in circles.

When Lenny stopped spinning, he got up and found that his whole body was shaking. "Oh my," he thought, "that cheetah is a fast runner." Then he added in rather a small voice, "But I'm still the bravest lion in Africa." He set off again across the plain. By now it was getting dark and Lenny was wishing he was at home with his mother and brothers and sisters. "I wonder if they've noticed I've gone," he thought sadly as a tear rolled down his furry cheek. He felt cold and tired and hungry as he crawled into the undergrowth to sleep.

Some time later Lenny was woken by a noise that was louder than anything he'd ever heard before – louder even than the elephant's trumpeting. It filled the night air and made the leaves

on the trees shake. The noise was getting louder and louder and the animal that was making it was getting nearer and nearer. Lenny peeped out from his hiding place and saw a huge golden creature with big yellow eyes that shone in the dark like lamps. It had a great crown of shaggy golden fur all around its head and its red jaws were open wide revealing a set of very large white fangs. How it roared! Lenny was terrified and about to turn tail and run, when the animal stopped roaring and spoke to him. "Come here, Lenny," said the animal gently. "It's me, your father, and I'm going to take you home. Climb up on my back, little one."

So Lenny climbed up on his father's back and was carried all the way home. And when they got there his father told his mother and his brothers and sisters that Lenny had been a very brave lion after all.

Little Tim and His Brother Sam

Little Tim was a very lucky boy. He had a lovely home, with the nicest parents you could hope for. He had a big yard, with a swing and a hockey net in it. And growing in the yard were lots of trees that you could climb and have adventures in. Little Tim even had a nice school, which he enjoyed going to every day and where he had lots of friends. In fact, almost everything in Tim's life was nice. Everything that is apart from one thing – Tim's brother Sam.

Sam was a very naughty boy. Worse still, whenever he got into mischief – which he did almost all of the time – he managed to make it look as though someone else was to blame. And that someone was usually poor Tim!

Once Sam thought that he would put salt in the sugar bowl instead of sugar. That afternoon, Sam and Tim's parents had some friends round for tea. All the guests put salt in their cups of tea, of course, thinking it was sugar. Well, being very polite they didn't like to say anything, even though their cups of tea tasted very strange indeed! When Sam and Tim's parents tasted their tea, however, they guessed immediately that someone had been playing a trick. They had to apologize to their guests and make them all fresh cups of tea. And who got the blame? Little Tim did, because Sam had sprinkled salt on Tim's bedroom floor so that their mother would think that Tim was the culprit.

Another time, Sam and Tim were playing soccer in the yard when Sam accidentally kicked the ball against a window and broke it. Sam immediately ran away and hid, so that when their father came out to investigate, only Tim was to be seen. So poor little Tim got the blame again.

Then there was the time when Sam and Tim's Aunt Jessica came to stay. She was a very nice lady, but she hated anything creepy-crawly, and as far as she was concerned that included frogs. So what did Sam do? Why, he went down to the lake and got a big, green frog to put in Aunt Jessica's purse. When Aunt Jessica opened her purse to get her glasses out, there staring out at her were two froggy eyes.

"Croak!" said the frog.

"Eeek!" yelled Aunt Jessica and almost jumped out of her skin.

"I told Tim not to do it," said Sam.

Tim opened his mouth and was just about to protest his innocence when his mother said, "Tim, go to your room immediately and don't come out until you are told."

Poor Tim went to his room and had to stay there until after supper. Sam thought it was very funny.

The next day, Sam decided that he would play another prank and blame it on Tim. He went to the shed and, one by one, took out all the garden tools. When he thought no-one was watching, he hid them all in Tim's bedroom cupboard. In went the spade, the fork, the watering can, the trowel – in fact, everything except the lawnmower. And the only reason that the lawnmower didn't go in was because it was too heavy to carry!

But this time, Sam's little prank was about to come unstuck, for Aunt Jessica had seen him creeping up the stairs to Tim's bedroom with the garden tools. She guessed immediately what Sam was up to, and who was likely to get the blame. When Sam wasn't about, she spoke to Tim. The two of them whispered to each other for a few seconds and then smiled triumphantly.

Later that day, Sam and Tim's father went to the shed to fetch some garden tools. Imagine his surprise when all he saw were some old flower pots and the lawnmower. He searched high and low for the garden tools. He looked behind the compost heap, under the steps, behind the sand pit and in the garage. But they weren't anywhere to be seen.

Then he started searching in the house. He looked in the kitchen cupboard, and was just looking under the stairs when something at the top of the stairs caught his eye. The handle from the garden spade was sticking out of the door to Sam's bedroom. Looking rather puzzled, he went upstairs and walked into Sam's bedroom. There, nestling neatly in the cupboard, were the rest of the tools.

"Sam, come up here immediately," called his father.

Sam, not realizing anything was amiss, came sauntering upstairs. Suddenly he saw all the garden tools that he had so carefully hidden in Tim's cupboard now sitting in *his* cupboard. He was speechless.

"Right," said his father, "before you go out to play, you can take all the tools back down to the shed. Then you can cut the grass. Then you can dig over the flower beds, and then you can do the weeding."

Well, it took Sam hours to do all the gardening. Tim and Aunt Jessica watched from the window and clutched their sides with laughter. Sam never did find out how all the garden tools found their way into his bedroom, but I think you've guessed, haven't you?

The Fox without a Tail

There was once a fine Fox, a most handsome fellow with a shiny red coat and a long bushy tail. This Fox was a rather vain creature and he spent long hours brushing his tail from top to tip until it shone like bright copper.

But one evening he had a most dreadful accident. As he hunted amongst the thickets and hedgerows for a tasty meal he suddenly heard a loud *clack!* and felt the most dreadful pain.

He realized at once that he had been caught in a trap and, pull as he might, his beautiful tail was stuck fast. Suddenly the pain stopped and to his great dismay the Fox found his tail lying in all its glory upon the ground. The trap had pulled it clean off. This was a calamity! Why, he was a Fox! The best and finest Fox that ever was — and what was a Fox without his tail? Why, little more than a laughing stock! How the other Foxes would taunt him when they saw him creeping by, tail-less. The very thought of it was more than he could bear.

After a while he stood up, collected his hat and made his way to the forest dell where the Foxes met for their nightly meetings. As the Fox strutted into the center of the circle a hushed silence fell on the entire company. He wore his best hat and tucked inside the hatband was his own fine red tail!

A young Fox began to titter, then another, then another, and soon the forest rang to the sounds of their rude laughter. With a dignified expression, the Fox held up his hand for silence and spoke.

"As you know, I have been blessed with a particularly fine specimen of a tail and I have been proud to carry it around behind me ever since I was born. But now I feel the time has come for a change. Tails should not drag behind us in the dirt. No, they should be worn on high, where their beauty can be fully admired."

The Fox paraded around the glade.

"This is the new fashion" he said "so you had all better start wearing your tails on your hats, like me."

Then an old Fox stood creakily to his feet.

"We have heard what you have to say, Brother Fox, but answer me this," he said. "Would you be quite so keen for us to follow this new fashion if your own tail had not been pulled off in a trap?" Then the poor Fox saw that everyone had seen through his cunning plan and he slunk off into the forest, much ashamed.

AND THE MORAL OF THIS STORY IS:
IF YOU SUFFER SOME MISFORTUNE, MAKE THE BEST OF
WHAT YOU HAVE AND DO NOT TRY TO
MAKE OTHERS SUFFER ALSO

The Dog and his Reflection

There was once a naughty Dog. He loved to sit outside the Butcher's shop and admire the strings of shiny sausages and rows of pink pork chops. How he wished he could help himself to something to eat!

One day when the Butcher's back was turned, the Dog ran into the shop and seized a large ham bone in his strong teeth. Off down the street he ran while the Butcher waved his sharpest knife and shouted after him angrily.

"Nobody has a bone as big and as tasty as mine!" the Dog said to himself as he set off for home. But as he crossed the bridge what should he see but another Dog with another bone — and this bone was just as big as his own! The Dog was astonished.

"I shall have that bone," he decided. "Two bones are better than one!" With that, the silly Dog opened his mouth and snapped greedily.

But what a shock he got when his own bone tumbled from his mouth and landed with a splash in the water. To the Dog's great dismay the bone sank quickly out of sight and he realized he was left with nothing at all.

Slowly he trudged back to his kennel, feeling very sorry for himself. He lay down and rested his head upon his paws. What a tragedy it was to have something in your grasp and then have it snatched suddenly away.

"I was wrong," sighed the Dog unhappily. "One bone is much, much better than none."

AND THE MORAL OF THIS STORY IS:
BE GRATEFUL FOR WHAT YOU HAVE

HOW THE CAMEL GOT HIS HUMP

Now this tale tells how the Camel got his big hump. In the beginning of years, when the world was so new-and-all, and the Animals were just beginning to work for Man, there lived a Camel, and he lived in the middle of a Howling Desert because he did not want to work.

He ate thorns and tamarisks and milkweed and prickles and was most 'scruciating idle, and when anybody spoke to him he said "Humph!" Just "Humph!" and no more. The Dog and the Horse and the Ox each tried to persuade him to help them with the work but the Camel would only reply "Humph!" Now the other animals thought that this was most unfair so when one day the Djinn of All Deserts came rolling along in a cloud of dust (Djinns always travel that way because it is Magic), they asked for help.

"Djinn of All Deserts," said the Horse, "is it right for any one to be idle, with the world so new-and-all? There is a thing in the middle of your Howling Desert with a long neck and long legs and he won't do a stroke of work."

Then the Djinn rolled across the desert until he found the Camel most 'scruciatingly idle, looking at his own reflection in a pool of water.

"You have given the Horse, the Dog and the Ox extra work, all on account of your 'scruciating idleness," said the Djinn sternly to the Camel.

"Humph!" the Camel replied.

"I shouldn't say that again if I was you," said the Djinn, and he began to work a Magic. Then the Camel said "Humph!" again; but no sooner had he said it than he saw his back begin to puff up and puff up into a great big lolloping humph.

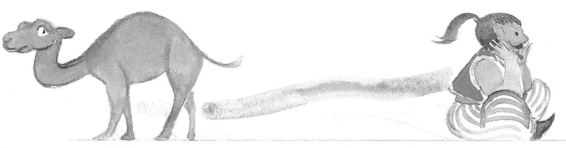

"That is your very own humph that you have brought upon your very own self by not working," said the Djinn. "In future you will be able to work and work and work for three whole days at a stretch without ever having to stop and eat, because now you can live off your humph."

Then the Camel humphed himself, humph and all, and went away to join the three Animals. And from that day to this the Camel always wears a Humph (but we call it a "hump" now, so as not to hurt his feelings).

THE ELEPHANT'S CHILD

In the High and Far-Off Times the Elephant, O Best Beloved, had no trunk. He had only a blackish, bulgy nose, as big as a boot, that he could wriggle about from side to side, but he couldn't pick up things with it. Now there was one Elephant, a new Elephant, an Elephant's Child, who was full of 'satiable curtiosity — and that means he asked ever so many questions. *And* he lived in Africa and he filled all Africa with his 'satiable curtiosities.

He asked his tall aunt, the Ostrich, why her tail-feathers grew just so. He asked his tall uncle, the Giraffe, what made his skin spotty. He asked his broad aunt, the Hippopotamus, why her eyes were red and he asked his hairy uncle, the Baboon, why melons tasted just so. He asked questions about everything that he saw, or heard, or felt, or smelt, or touched, and his aunts and his uncles spanked and spanked him but *still* he was full of 'satiable curtiosity!

One fine morning the Elephant's Child asked a new fine question that he had never asked before.

"What does the Crocodile have for dinner?" he said. Then everybody said "Hush!" and spanked him well.

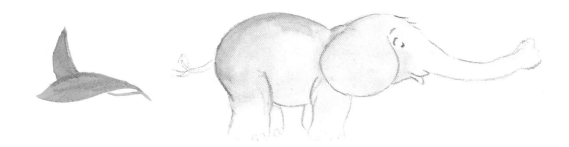

When they had quite finished, the Elephant's Child came upon Kolokolo Bird sitting in a thorn bush.

"If you want to find out what the Crocodile has for dinner," said the Bird, "you must go to the banks of the great gray-green, greasy Limpopo River, all set about with fever-trees, and there you will find out." So the Elephant's Child set off to find the Crocodile. Now you must understand, O Best Beloved, that this 'satiable Elephant's Child had never seen a Crocodile, and did not know what one was like.

But nevertheless he set off for the Limpopo River and the first thing that he found was a Bi-Colored-Python-Rock-Snake curled round a rock.

"'Scuse me," said the Elephant's Child most politely, "but have you seen such a thing as a Crocodile in these promiscuous parts?"

Then the Bi-Coloured-Python-Rock-Snake uncoiled himself very quickly from the rock, and spanked the Elephant's Child with his scalesome, flailsome tail, and when he had finished the Elephant's Child thanked him politely and continued on his way.

After a while he trod on what he thought was a log of wood at the very edge of the great gray-green, greasy Limpopo River, but it was really the Crocodile, O Best Beloved, and the Crocodile winked one eye — like this!

"'Scuse me," said the Elephant's Child most politely, "but do you happen to have seen a Crocodile in these promiscuous parts?"

Then the Crocodile winked the other eye, and lifted half his tail out of the mud, and the Elephant's Child stepped back most politely, because he did not wish to be spanked again.

"Come hither, Little One," said the Crocodile. "Why do you ask me such things?"

"'Scuse me," said the Elephant's Child, "but all my aunts and uncles have spanked me and the Bi-Colored-Python-Rock-Snake has spanked me and so, if it's all the same to you, I don't want to be spanked again."

"Come hither, Little One," said the Crocodile, "for I am the Crocodile," and he wept crocodile-tears to show it was quite true. Then the Elephant's Child grew all breathless, and panted, and then he spoke.

"You are the very person I have been looking for all these long days. Will you please tell me what you have for dinner?"

"Come hither, Little One," said the Crocodile, "and I'll whisper."

Then the Elephant's Child put his head down close to the Crocodile's musky, tusky mouth, and the Crocodile caught him by his little nose, which up to that moment had been no bigger than a boot.

"I think," said the Crocodile from between his teeth, like this, "I think today I will begin with Elephant's Child!" and he pulled and he pulled and he pulled.

"Led go!" said the Elephant's Child. "You are hurtig me!" Then the Bi-Colored-Python-Rock-Snake scuffled down the bank and knotted himself in a double-clove-hitch around the Elephant's Child's legs.

And he pulled, and the Elephant's Child pulled, and the Crocodile pulled — but the Elephant's Child and the Bi-Colored-Python-Rock-Snake pulled hardest (and by this time the poor nose was nearly five feet long!)

At last the Crocodile let go of the Elephant's Child's nose with a plop that you could hear all up and down the Limpopo. Then the Elephant's child dangled his poor pulled nose in the water.

"I am waiting for it to shrink," he explained.

There he sat for three days patiently waiting for his nose to shrink back to its usual size but the long stretched nose never grew any shorter. For, O Best Beloved, you will see and understand that the Crocodile had pulled it out into a really truly trunk same as all Elephants have today.

At the end of the third day a fly came and stung him on the shoulder and before he knew what he was doing he lifted up his trunk and hit that fly dead with the end of it. Later he grew hungry, so almost without thinking he put out his trunk and plucked a large bundle of grass and stuffed it in his mouth.

"The sun is very hot here," said the Elephant's Child, and before he thought what he was doing he schlooped up a schloop of mud from the banks of the river and he slapped it on his head where it made a cool schloopy-sloshy mud cap all trickly behind his ears.

Then the Elephant's Child went home across Africa and how proud he was of his useful new nose. And the first thing he did when he saw all his relations was to spank them with his long trunk — and after that, none of them dared spank anyone ever again!

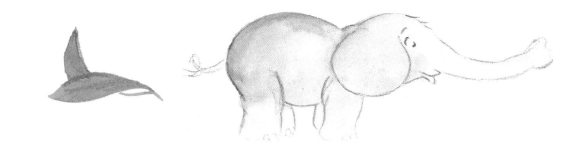

BRER RABBIT AND THE PEANUT PATCH

Brer Fox was mighty proud of his peanut patch. He weeded it and watered it and looked forward very much to the day when he could eat a fine crop of nuts. But Brer Rabbit had his eye on that self same peanut patch and one morning, when the peanuts had grown big and ripe, he crept through the fence and helped himself just as sassy as you please.

When Brer Fox saw that somebody had been scrabbling in and out of his plants he grew mighty mad

"I'm going to make a trap and catch that no-good varmint who's stealing my peanuts if it's the last thing I do," he said to himself. Soon he had made a fine trap with some rope and a slim hickory sapling and he positioned it right next to the hole in the fence.

The very next day Brer Rabbit came sashaying down the road towards the peanut patch. He wriggled all unsuspecting through the hole in the fence and what a fright he got when he suddenly found himself whisked up in the air and dangling by his back paws on the end of a rope! There he swung, to and fro, while he tried his best to think of a way to free himself.

Just then Brer Bear came ambling down the road. "Howdy, Brer Bear!" called Brer Rabbit.

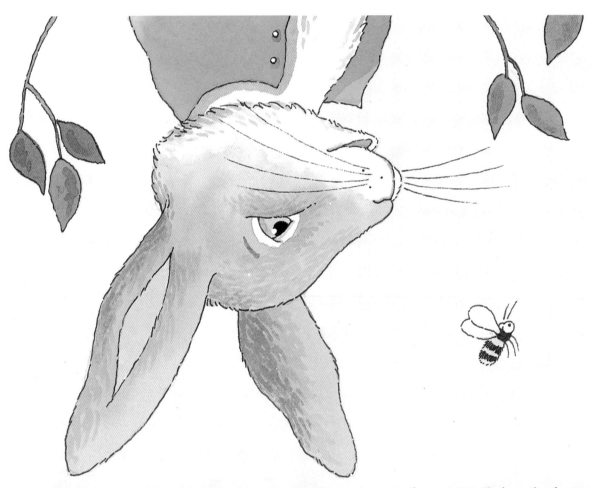

"What in tarnation are you doin' up there?" asked the astonished Bear as he spotted Brer Rabbit above him.

"Why, I'm earning a dollar a minute guarding the peanut patch for Brer Fox," replied the wily Rabbit. "But I reckon I've earned enough money now," he added. "Do you want to take over from me?"

Brer Bear looked at him doubtfully. "Do you reckon I could do it?" he said. Brer Rabbit nodded encouragingly.

"Why, it's easy as pie," he said. "I'll show you what to do!"

Soon Brer Rabbit was standing on the ground and Brer Bear was swinging in the air.

"Brer Fox, come out!" shouted the naughty Rabbit. "Here's the rascal who's been stealing your peanuts!" Out shot Brer Fox with a stout stick in his hand.

"So that's your game, is it?" he cried, and he set about poor Brer Bear with his stick. The Bear tried in vain to explain that he was guarding his peanut patch for him but the furious Brer Fox did not believe a single word of it.

And where was Brer Rabbit? Why, he was long gone. Long gone!

POOR LITTLE TED

Poor little Ted
Fell out of bed,
And found that he had
A big bump on his head!

He let out a scream,
I woke from my dream,
And soon made him better
With cake and ice-cream!

IN A SPIN

I had a little teddy,
He went everywhere with me,
But now I've gone and lost him,
Oh, where can my teddy be?

I've looked behind the sofa,
I've looked beneath the bed,
I've looked out in the garden,
And in the garden shed!

I've looked inside the bathtub,
And underneath my chair,
Oh, where, oh, where is Teddy?
I've hunted everywhere!

At last I try the kitchen,
My face breaks in a grin.
There's Teddy in the washtub –
Mom's sent him for a spin!

279

BIRTHDAY BUNNIES

"It's my first birthday tomorrow!" announced Snowy, a little white rabbit, very proudly. "Isn't that exciting?"

"Yes, very exciting!" said Whiskers, her brother. "Because it's my birthday too!"

"And mine!" said Patch.

"And mine!" said Nibble.

"And mine!" said Twitch.

"Do you think mom and dad have got a surprise for us?" asked Snowy.

"I hope so!" said Whiskers.

"Me too!" said Patch.

"Me too!" said Nibble.

"Me too!" said Twitch.

Mrs Rabbit was listening outside the door, as her children were getting ready for bed. She heard the little bunnies chattering excitedly about their birthdays the next day.

Whatever could she do to make it a special day for them? She sat and thought very hard, and later that evening, when Mr Rabbit came home, she said: "It is the childrens' first birthday tomorrow, and I'm planning a surprise for them. I want to make them a carrot cake, but I will need some carrots. Could you go and dig some nice fresh ones up from your vegetable garden?"

"Certainly, dear," said Mr Rabbit, and off he went back outside.

Mr Rabbit was proud of the carrots he grew. They were very fine carrots, crunchy and sweet and delicious. Every year he entered them in the Country Show, and they nearly always won first prize. So you can imagine his dismay when he arrived at his vegetable patch to find that every single carrot had been dug up and stolen!

He marched back inside. "Someone has stolen my carrots!" he announced to his wife, crossly. "And I am going to find out just who it is!"

And although it was getting late, he went back outside, and set off to find the naughty person.

First of all he stopped at Hungry Hare's house, and knocked at the door.

"Someone has stolen my carrots!" Mr Rabbit said. "Do you know who?"

"Oh, yes," said Hungry Hare. "But it wasn't me." And although Mr Rabbit pressed him, Hungry Hare would say no more.

Next Mr Rabbit went to Sly Fox's house.

"Someone has stolen my carrots!" he said. "Do you know who?"

"Oh, yes," said Sly Fox. "But it wasn't me." And although Mr Rabbit begged and pleaded with him, Sly Fox would say no more.

So Mr Rabbit marched to Bill Badger's house, and asked if he knew who had taken the carrots.

"Why, yes, in fact I do," said Bill Badger. "But it wasn't me."

And just like the others, he would say no more. It was the same wherever Mr Rabbit went, and although he got very cross, and stamped his foot, no one would tell him who had stolen his carrots!

"You'll find out soon enough," said Red Squirrel.

So Mr Rabbit went home feeling very puzzled.

"It seems that everyone knows who it was, but no one will tell me!" said Mr Rabbit to his wife.

"Not everyone, dear," she said. "I don't know who it was either. All I know is that it's our childrens' first birthday tomorrow, and we have no surprise for them." And feeling very miserable and confused, they went to bed, determined to get to the bottom of the mystery in the morning.

Next day the little bunnies came running into the kitchen, where their parents were having breakfast.

"Happy birthday, everyone!" called Snowy.

"Happy birthday!" cried the other little bunnies.

"Now, it's not much, but I wanted to give each of you a surprise!" Snowy went on. "By the way, I hope you don't mind, Dad." And with that Snowy pulled out a box of juicy carrots, each tied with a bow, and handed one to each of her brothers and sisters.

"Snap!" cried Whiskers, "I had just the same idea!" and he pulled out another box of carrots.

"Me too!" said Patch.

"Me too!" said Nibble.

"Me too!" said Twitch.

Soon there was a great pile of juicy carrots heaped on the kitchen table.

"So that's what happened to my carrots!" cried Mr Rabbit, in amazement. "I thought they had been stolen! And when he told the little bunnies the story they laughed till their sides ached. Then Mrs Rabbit put on her apron and shooed them outside.

"Just leave the carrots with me," she said.
"I have a birthday surprise of my own in store!"

And so the mystery was solved. It turned out
that Hungry Hare had seen the little bunnies
creep out one by one, and each dig up a few
carrots when they thought no one was looking.
He knew it was their birthdays and he guessed
what they were doing. He had told the other forest
folk, and everyone thought it was a great joke.

Mr Rabbit felt very ashamed that he had been so cross with everyone, when they were really just keeping the secret. To apologise, he invited them for a special birthday tea that afternoon, which the little bunnies thought was a great surprise.

And of course the highlight of the day was when Mrs Rabbit appeared from the kitchen carrying, what else, but an enormous carrot cake!

NIPPY SNIPPY

Eeeny, meeny, miney, mo,
Here comes Crab to pinch your toe!
Shout out loud and he'll let go -
Eeeny, meeny, miney, mo!

Nippy, snippy, snappy, snip,
Be careful when you take a dip,
Or Crab will catch you in his grip!
Nippy, snippy, snappy, snip!

ACHOO!

Mouse's eyes filled up with water,
His little nose started to twitch,
A tingling tickled his whiskers,
And then his knees started to itch.

He got a bad case of the hiccups,
Then threw back his head in a sneeze,
And he said, "I'm most awfully sorry,
It's just I'm allergic to cheese!"

Ten Little Men

Ten little men standing straight,
Ten little men open the gate,
Ten little men all in a ring,

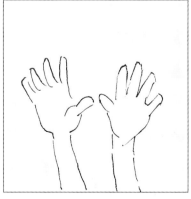

Hold up ten fingers

TEN LITTLE MEN...

Turn wrists

OPEN THE GATE...

Make fingers into ring

ALL IN A RING...

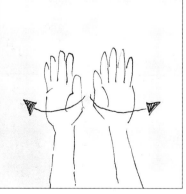

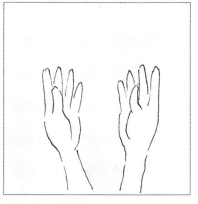

Ten little men bow to the king,
Ten little men dance all day,
Ten little men hide away.

Bend fingers

Dance fingers

Hide hands behind back

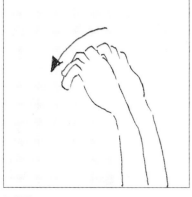

BOW...

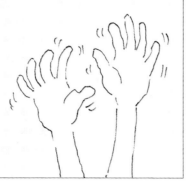

DANCE...

HIDE AWAY

Incy Wincy Spider

Incy Wincy Spider climbing up the spout,
Down came the rain and washed the spider out.
Out came the sun, and dried up all the rain,
Incy Wincy Spider climbed up the spout again.

Touch opposite index fingers and
thumbs together by twisting wrists

CLIMBING UP THE SPOUT...

Wiggle fingers as you lower them

DOWN CAME THE RAIN...

Make a big circle with arms.
Repeat first action.

OUT CAME THE SUN...

294

London Bridge is Falling Down

London bridge is falling down,
Falling down, falling down,
London bridge is falling down,
My fair lady.

Build it up with wood and clay,
Wood and clay, wood and clay,
Build it up with wood and clay,
My fair lady

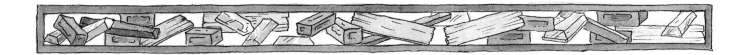

Wood and clay will wash away,
Wash away, wash away,
Wood and clay will wash away,
My fair lady.

Build it up with bricks and mortar,
Bricks and mortar, bricks and mortar,
Build it up with bricks and mortar,
My fair lady.

Bricks and mortar will not stay,
Will not stay, will not stay,
Bricks and mortar will not stay,
My fair lady.

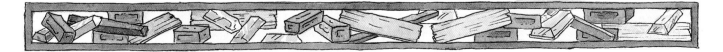

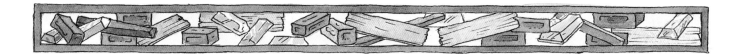

Build it up with iron and steel,
Iron and steel, iron and steel,
Build it up with iron and steel,
My fair lady.

Iron and steel will bend and bow,
Bend and bow, bend and bow
Iron and steel will bend and bow,
My fair lady.

Build it up with silver and gold,
Silver and gold, silver and gold,
Build it up with silver and gold,
My fair lady.

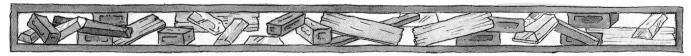

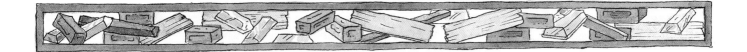

Silver and gold will be stolen away,
Stolen away, stolen away,
Silver and gold will be stolen away,
My fair lady.

Set a man to watch all night,
Watch all night, watch all night,
Set a man to watch all night,
My fair lady.

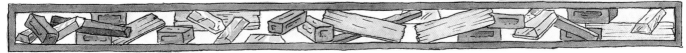

Granny Casts a Spell

Susie was very fond of her Granny. Each day, when Susie got home from school, Granny was always there sitting by the fire knitting. Granny knitted so fast that sometimes it seemed as though the knitting needles sparked in the firelight.

"Do you know," Granny would say, "that I'm really a witch?" Susie always laughed when Granny said that because she didn't look at all like a witch. She had a smiling face and kind eyes and she never wore black. Not ever. When Granny wasn't looking, Susie would take a peek inside her wardrobe just in case she might find a broomstick or a witch's hat. But she never found so much as a book of spells.

"I don't believe you're a witch," said Susie.

"I am," replied Granny, "and I'll cast a spell one day. You'll know when that day comes, for my needles will start to knit by themselves." After that, Susie kept a careful watch over Granny's needles, but they always lay quite still in the basket of knitting.

One day, Susie was playing in her yard when she heard the sound of weeping. The sound seemed to be coming from under the old tree in the corner. She walked towards the tree and as she did so the crying noise got louder, but she could not see anyone there. Then she looked down at her feet and there – sitting on a mossy stone – was a tiny little man. He was neatly dressed in a yellow velvet waistcoat and knickerbockers. On his feet were beautiful, shiny, buckled shoes, and a three-cornered hat with a wren's feather in it trembled on his shaking head. When the little man saw Susie, he stopped crying and started to dab his eyes with a fine lace handkerchief.

"Whatever can the matter be?" asked Susie, crouching down.

"Oh dear, oh dear!" sobbed the little man, "I am the fairy princess's tailor and she has asked me to make her a lovely gown to wear to the May Ball tonight, but a wicked elf has played a

301

trick on me and turned all my fine gossamer fabric into bats'
wings. Now I shall never be able to make the princess's gown
and she will be very angry with me." He started to cry again.

"Don't cry!" said Susie. "I'm sure I can help. My Granny's
got a sewing basket full of odds and ends. I'll see if she's got
anything nice for a party dress. I'm sure she won't mind
sparing some – after all, you won't need much," she said.
At that, the little man looked a bit more cheerful.

"Wait here," said Susie, "while I run indoors and see."
She ran up the garden path and in through the back door.

"Granny, Granny!" she called. She ran into the sitting room
expecting to find Granny knitting by the fire. But Granny had
her eyes closed and she was whispering to herself. On her lap was
her knitting – and the needles were moving all by themselves,
so that the yarn danced up and down on the old lady's knees.

For a moment, Susie was too astounded to move. Then she thought, "I hope Granny's not casting a bad spell. I'd better make sure the little tailor is alright."

She ran back down the garden path and there under the tree sat the tailor, surrounded by a great pile of gorgeous gossamer, shining in the sunlight.

"I've never seen such fine material – ever!" he exclaimed. "But where did it come from? I just closed my eyes to dab them with my handkerchief and when I opened them again – there it was!"

"I don't know," said Susie, "but I think my Granny might have had something to do with it."

"Well, I'll never be able to thank her enough," said the tailor. "For now I shall be able to make the finest gown in the whole of fairyland. The princess will dance the night away in the prettiest dress there ever was." He paused and then went on, "I'm also indebted to you, for it was you who helped me in the first place. I would like it very much if you came to the May Ball, too."

"Why, thank you so much," Susie replied, "I should like that very much." She didn't want to hurt the tailor's feelings but she knew she couldn't go – she was far too big to go to a fairy ball!

"Well I must get on with the dress now," said the little man, reaching for a pair of fairy scissors. "See you tonight!" And with that he vanished.

Susie went indoors again. Granny was knitting by the fire as usual. Susie wondered if she had dreamed the whole thing. Everything seemed so normal. Really, how could she have imagined she'd seen a fairy tailor in the garden! And as for Granny casting a spell!

That night, Susie lay in bed and wondered if the fairies really were having a ball. How she longed to be there! Once she thought she heard a tapping at the window. Was that the fairy tailor she saw through the glass – or was she imagining it? In the middle of the night she awoke with a start. There was a click, clicking noise at the end of her bed.

"Granny is that you?" called Susie.

"Yes, dear," replied Granny. "I couldn't sleep, so I decided to do some knitting. All at once the needles started twitching, so I knew it was time to cast a spell. What is your wish, Susie?"

"I... I...," stammered Susie, "I want to go to the May Ball," she blurted.

"Then you shall, my dear," said Granny.

In an instant, Susie felt herself shrinking and when she looked down she saw she was wearing a beautiful gown and tiny satin slippers. Then she floated on gossamer wings out through the window and off to the Ball.

The next morning, Susie woke up in her bed. Had it all been a dream – the revelry, the fairy food, the frog band, the dance with the fairy prince? Then she saw something peeping out from under her pillow. And what do you think it was? It was a tiny, tiny shred of the finest gossamer fabric.

Peter Meets a Dragon

Once upon a time there was a young boy named Peter. He lived in an ordinary house with an ordinary mom and dad, an ordinary sister and an ordinary pet cat, called Jasper. In fact, everything in Peter's life was so ordinary that he sometimes wished that something extraordinary would happen. "Why doesn't a giant come and squash the house flat with his foot?" he wondered, and "If only a pirate would take my sister hostage!" But each day, Peter would wake up in the morning and everything was just the same as it had been the day before.

One morning Peter woke up to find a very strange smell in the house. Looking out of his bedroom window, he saw that the front lawn was scorched and blackened. There was smoke drifting off the grass and, further away, he could see some bushes ablaze.

Peter rushed downstairs and out of the front door. He ran out of the yard and down the street following the trail of smoke and burning grass. He grew more and more puzzled, however, as there was no sign of anything that could have caused such a blaze.

Peter was about to run home and tell his mum and dad, when he heard a panting noise coming from the undergrowth. Parting the bushes gently with his hands he found a young creature. It had green, scaly skin, a pair of wings and a long snout full of sharp teeth. Every now and again a little tongue of flame came from its nostrils, setting the grass around it on fire. "A baby dragon!" Peter said to himself, in great surprise. Big tears were rolling out of the dragon's yellow eyes and down its scaly cheeks as it flapped its wings desperately and tried to take off.

When the dragon saw Peter it stopped flapping its wings. "Oh, woe is me!" it sobbed. "Where am I?"

"Where do you want to be?" asked Peter, kneeling down on the scorched ground.

"I want to be in Dragonland with my friends," replied the dragon. "We were all flying together, but I just couldn't keep up with them. I got tired and needed a rest. I called to the others but they didn't hear me. Then I just had to stop and get my breath back. Now I don't know where I am, or if I'll ever see my friends again!" And with that the baby dragon started to cry once more.

"I'm sure I can help. I'll get you home," said Peter, though he had no idea how.

"You?" hissed a voice nearby. "How could you possibly help? You're just a boy!" Peter looked round, and to his astonishment found Jasper sitting behind him. "I suppose you're going to wave a magic wand, are you?" continued Jasper. "You need to call in an expert." Then he turned his back on Peter and the baby dragon and started washing his paws.

Peter was astounded. He'd never heard Jasper talking before. He had thought he was just an ordinary pet cat. "W… w… what do you mean?" he stammered.

"Well," said Jasper, glancing over his shoulder at Peter, "I reckon that horse over there could help. Follow me."

So Peter and the baby dragon – whose name was Flame – followed Jasper over to where the horse stood at the edge of a field. Jasper leaped up on to the gate and called to the horse. Then he whispered in the horse's ear. The horse thought for a moment, then whispered back in Jasper's ear. "He says he's got a friend on the other side of the wood who'll help," said Jasper.

"But how?" asked Peter, looking perplexed.

"Be patient! Follow me!" said Jasper as he stalked off through the grass. "And tell your friend to stop setting fire to everything!" he added. Peter saw, to his horror, that Flame was indeed blazing a trail through the field.

"I can't help it," cried Flame, about to burst into tears again. "Every time I get out of breath I start to pant, and then I start breathing fire."

"Let me carry you," said Peter. He picked Flame up in his arms and ran after Jasper. The baby dragon felt very strange. His body was all cold and clammy, but his mouth was still breathing hot smoke, which made Peter's eyes water.

He ran through the wood, just keeping Jasper's upright tail in sight. On the other side of the wood was another field, and in the field was a horse. But this was no ordinary horse. Peter stopped dead in his tracks and stared. The horse was pure milky white, and from its head grew a single, long horn. "A unicorn!" breathed Peter.

Jasper was already talking to the unicorn. He beckoned with his paw to Peter. "He'll take your friend home and you can go, too, Peter, but don't be late for supper, or you know what your mother will say." And with that, Jasper was off.

"Climb aboard," said the unicorn gently.

Peter and the little dragon scrambled up on to the unicorn's back. "What an adventure," thought Peter. Up, up, and away they soared through the clouds.

Flame held tightly on to Peter's hand with his clammy paw. At last Peter could see a mountain ahead through the clouds. Now they were descending through the clouds again, and soon the unicorn landed right at the top of the mountain. "I'm home!" squeaked Flame happily as they landed.

Sure enough, several dragons were running over to greet him. They looked quite friendly, but some of them were rather large and one was breathing a great deal of fire.

"Time for me to go," said Peter a little nervously, as Flame jumped off the unicorn's back and flew to the ground. The unicorn took off again and soon they were back in the field once more.

As he slid off the unicorn's back, Peter turned to thank him, but when he looked he saw that it was just an ordinary horse with no trace of a horn at all. Peter walked back home across the field, but there was no sign of burnt grass. He reached his own front lawn, which was also in perfect condition. Peter felt more and more perplexed. "I hope Jasper can explain," he thought, as the cat ran past him and into the house. "Jasper, I took the baby dragon home. What's happened to the burnt grass?" he blurted out. But Jasper said not a word. He ignored Peter and curled up in his basket.

When Peter wasn't looking, however, Jasper gave him a glance that seemed to say, "Well, was that a big enough adventure for you?"

Puss in Boots

Once upon a time in France, there lived a miller who had three sons. When he died, the miller left the mill to his eldest son. To his second son he left a donkey on whose back sacks of flour could be loaded and delivered to customers. But to the youngest son, who was much the most handsome of the three, he left only a large cat, whose job it had been to chase the mice that came at night to make holes in the sacks and steal grain.

The poor youngest brother wondered how on earth he would make his living with only the cat for company. He could see that he would have to go out into the world to seek his fortune. "I shall have to leave you behind, Puss," he said, "for I don't see how I am to look after you."

"What about if I looked after *you?*" replied Puss.

"Whatever do you mean?" said his master.

"I can make your fortune for you," said the cat. "All I need is a large drawstring bag and a pair of really smart boots – for my hind feet."

Well, the boy was mighty puzzled, but he decided it was worth letting the cat try to win his fortune, as he surely had no idea of what to do otherwise. With his brand new boots on his hind paws and his drawstring bag slung over his shoulder, Puss set off with nothing but a handful of corn from the mill.

The first thing he did was go straight to the nearest rabbit warren where he opened the bag, put a little corn into it and laid it open near the rabbit hole. Then Puss laid in wait until dusk, when the rabbits came out of their hole. One rabbit came up, full of curiosity, and hopped into the bag to get the corn. Up sprang Puss and pulled the drawstring tight. Then, instead of taking the rabbit to his master, he set off to the palace, where he announced that he had brought the king a present.

"Your Majesty," said Puss, taking a low bow, "I am a messenger from the Marquis of Carabas, your neighbor. He was out hunting today and was lucky enough to catch a fine young rabbit. He begs that you will accept it as a present."

The king was puzzled, because he'd never heard of this Marquis, but he was pleased to have the rabbit. "Tell your master that I am delighted with his kind present," he said.

Day after day, Puss went out hunting in this manner and each time he presented his catch to the king. "Don't forget," he said to his master, "that you're supposed to be a Marquis." The young boy had no idea what the cat was talking about, but he trusted him nevertheless. After a while the cat started to be invited in for a drink and a chat with the guards and he soon got to know all the court gossip. One time, Puss got to hear that the king was planning to drive the next day in his grand carriage with his daughter, the most beautiful princess in France. Puss took care to find out which direction they intended to take.

The next morning he said to his master, "I think it would be a good idea to take a swim in the river this morning." The boy agreed and, by the look in Puss's eye, he knew that he had a plan in mind. Puss led the way to a part of the river where the royal carriage was bound to pass. While the boy was swimming in the river, Puss heard the sound of the approaching carriage. Quickly Puss hid his master's ragged clothes under a stone and as the carriage came into view he ran into the road shouting, "Help! The Marquis of Carabas is drowning!" At once the king recognised Puss and ordered his guards to go to the rescue. The boy pretended to be drowning, so that the guards had quite a struggle to get him to the bank.

Meanwhile, Puss went up to the carriage, bowed to the king and said, "While he was bathing, thieves unfortunately stole my master's fine clothing. He cannot appear before your daughter without any clothes."

"Of course not," replied the king, and sent his footman to fetch a spare set of clothes from the back of the royal carriage. Now that the handsome boy was properly dressed, the king was glad to meet the mysterious Marquis, of whom he had heard so much from Puss. He welcomed the 'Marquis' into the carriage, where he sat next to the princess. "Come for a drive with us, my dear Marquis," said the king.

Without another word Puss set off and disappeared around the next bend of the road. By the time the king's gilded carriage was on its way again, Puss was a long way ahead. Soon he passed a field of haymakers. "My good haymakers," said Puss, "you must tell the king that this meadow belongs to the Marquis of Carabas – or I'll grind you all to little pieces."

Now Puss knew that the meadow really belonged to an ogre, who was known to be able to change his shape. So of course the haymakers had no idea if this was just an ordinary pussy cat telling them what to do – or if it really was the ogre. Soon the royal carriage passed by and the king leaned out and asked to whom the field belonged. "To the Marquis of Carabas, your Majesty," chorused the haymakers.

"That's a fine piece of land you've got there," said the king, nudging the boy who was busy chatting to the princess.

All along the road it was the same story. Puss always got there before the royal carriage. Woodcutters, shepherds, and farmers all told the king that their master was the Marquis of Carabas, because Puss had threatened to turn them all into mincemeat if they didn't. Now Puss caught sight of a fine castle which he recognised as belonging to the ogre.

Puss went up to the great gate and asked to speak to the ogre. Puss said to him, "I heard that you can transform yourself in the most amazing way – into a lion for example. But I really can't believe that this is true."

The ogre was so offended that he bellowed, "JUST YOU WATCH!" and instantly turned himself into a lion. Puss pretended to be scared and jumped up on to the castle roof. The ogre turned himself back into an ogre. "That'll teach you," he roared.

"You gave me a dreadful fright," said Puss. "Do you know, people say you can even turn yourself into a tiny animal, such as rat or mouse. But that's absurd. It's quite impossible."

"IMPOSSIBLE, EH?" screeched the ogre, and the great foolish creature turned himself into a mouse.

In an instant, Puss had pounced on him and gobbled him up, bones and all. At that moment, the royal carriage rumbled over the drawbridge, for the king, too, had spotted the castle and wondered who lived there.

"Welcome to the castle of the Marquis of Carabas, your Majesty," said Puss, who had just wiped the last morsels of the ogre from his whiskers.

"What," cried the king, turning to the young boy, "is this yours, too?" The boy glanced at Puss and then nodded. "May we see inside?" asked the king.

So the king, the princess and the miller's son looked around the castle. And very fine it was, too. The ogre's servants were so happy to see the back of their master that they laid on a fine feast. And at the end of the meal, the king agreed to give his daughter's hand in marriage to the 'Marquis'.

As for Puss, his master was so grateful that he saw to it that the cat was made a lord. So they all lived happily ever after and Puss never had to chase another mouse for the rest of his life.

Hansel and Grettel

Once upon a time long ago there lived a poor woodcutter and his two children, Hansel and Grettel. The children's mother had died when they were very young and their father had married again. Their stepmother was a wicked woman and she did not love Hansel and Grettel. The woodcutter had very little money to spend on food and so all four of them went hungry for much of the week.

Late one night as the two children lay shivering in their beds they heard their stepmother talking.

"Something must be done or we will all starve to death," the woman whispered to the children's father. "We have enough food for two mouths, but not for four. We must get rid of Hansel and Grettel."

Grettel wept bitterly as she heard her stepmother describe how she would lead the children deep into the forest and leave them there to perish.

"I will find a way home, little sister," said Hansel.

The next morning the children were taken far away.

"Stay here until we return," said their stepmother. Soon night fell and they were left quite alone.

Poor Grettel sobbed as if her heart would break.

"Dry your eyes, little sister," said Hansel. "On the way here I dropped a white pebble on the ground every few steps. See how they shine in the moonlight. We can follow the trail home." Sure enough, the pebbles showed them the way perfectly and some hours later they were pushing open the door of their house.

Their father was overjoyed to see them for he had bitterly regretted agreeing to his wife's plan. Their stepmother pretended she was pleased but they could clearly see the disappointment on her face.

Some days later Hansel and Grettel heard her talking to their father once more.

"We are hungrier than ever," she complained. "We must try and lose the children again tomorrow." This time Hansel did not have time to collect a pocketful of white pebbles so when they were led into the forest he dropped a trail of crumbled bread for them to follow that night. But when they searched for the crumbs they were dismayed to find them all gone, for the birds had eaten every one!

"We are lost!" cried Grettel.

Again and again they tried to find a way out of the forest but every path they took led them ever deeper into the wood. Suddenly Hansel saw a white dove sitting upon a branch. She twittered at them, then flew off over the trees.

"I believe she is telling us to follow her," said Hansel and with weary steps they trudged after the little bird. She sang as if to encourage them on their way and after a time they found themselves in an open glade. And there in the middle of the clearing was the most perfect little gingerbread cottage.

"Oh, Hansel!" gasped Grettel. "The roof is made of honey cake and the windows are made of barley sugar! I must just nibble a little corner." Soon they were both munching away on their favorite bits of the house and nothing had ever tasted quite so delicious.

All of a sudden the door flew open and out hobbled an old dame leaning upon a stick. The children drew back in fear but the old lady smiled at them kindly.

"Welcome to my home, my dears," she said. "Come inside and I will look after you." She fed them sweet pancakes, then put them to bed under cosy quilts.

But when Hansel and Grettel awoke next day the old lady's kind manner had changed. Her weak eyes glinted cruelly as she grabbed Hansel by the arm.

"You will make a tasty morsel for me to eat," she cackled and then the children saw that they had been tricked. The old lady was a witch and she meant to make a meal of them! Laughing cruelly, she bundled Hansel into a cage.

"I will fatten you up before I cook you," she hissed and Hansel shook with fear. Every day she checked to see how fat he was getting but clever Hansel stuck an old bone through the bars and when the old crone pinched it, she decided he was still too thin to eat.

At last the witch could wait no longer.

"Fat or thin, I will eat him as he is," she decided, clutching at Grettel with one claw-like hand. "And you will help me prepare the cooking pot."

How the little girl sobbed as she carried the water and lit the fire under the oven. The witch scowled at her and stamped her feet.

"Stop your wailing," she shouted. "Just climb in the oven and tell me how hot it is." Then Grettel had a clever idea. She looked up at the Witch timidly.

"I don't know how to climb inside the oven," she said anxiously. "Can you show me?"

The witch stamped her foot again, but moved close to the oven entrance.

"Why, you silly goose," she said crossly, "it is perfectly simple. All you have to do is put one foot here and then you can step right inside." But as the witch showed her where to put her feet Grettel suddenly ran at her and with a great shove pushed the old hag right inside the oven and slammed the iron door tight shut. Gracious, how the old witch yelled! Soon Hansel was free from the cage and jumping for joy.

Then the two children explored every inch of the gingerbread cottage, upstairs and down and hidden in every corner were chests full of treasure. Jewels and pearls, gold and silver — the children could hardly believe their eyes! They filled their pockets to the brim and little Grettel held as much as she could hold in her apron.

Soon they were ready and they set off to find their way home. After a while they came to a large lake but they could find no way of crossing the water.

"Now we will never see Father again," sighed Hansel, but just then a large white duck came swimming by.

"I will carry you over on my back," she offered and so the two grateful children were delivered safe to the other side. For many hours they walked under the shade of the trees and after a time the forest began to look more familiar and then, to their delight, Hansel and Grettel saw their own little home in front of them.

Their father wept for joy as he gathered the children into his arms for he had not had a single happy hour since he had lost them.

"Your wicked stepmother has gone away for good," he said. "Now we will be together forever.

THE THREE BILLY GOATS GRUFF
Illustrated by Martin Aitchinson

Once upon a time in a land far away there lived three Billy Goats. There was a large Billy Goat, a middle-sized Billy Goat and a small Billy Goat. They were the Three Billy Goats Gruff.

They lived high up on a rocky mountainside and leapt from peak to peak in search of food. But they found very little grass and often went to sleep with their empty tummies rumbling with hunger.

"We will look for a better place to live," decided the oldest Billy Goat at last. "Somewhere with plenty of good, sweet grass to eat."

Soon they had reached the valley far below.

"That is the place for us," said the oldest Billy Goat and he nodded his head at a lush green meadow on the other side of a swift mountain stream. Now the only way to cross that stream was over a rickety wooden bridge and under that rickety wooden bridge lived the ugliest, fiercest troll that ever was. He liked nothing better than to gobble up goats for his supper. But the smallest Billy Goat Gruff stamped his hoof and set off over the bridge, trip, trap, trip, trap.

"Who's that trip-trapping over my bridge?" roared the troll and the little Billy Goat stood stock-still.

338

"It is me, the smallest Billy Goat Gruff," he said. "I am off to the meadow to eat the sweet grass."

"Oh, no, you are not!" roared the troll, "for I am going to eat you all up!"

"But I am small and bony," replied the smallest Billy Goat. "You should wait for my brother. He is much fatter than me." The troll scratched his head and the smallest Billy Goat Gruff quickly trotted over the bridge and was soon safe on the other side. Then the middle-sized Billy Goat Gruff began to cross the bridge.

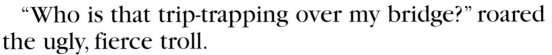

"Who is that trip-trapping over my bridge?" roared the ugly, fierce troll.

"It is me, the middle-sized Billy Goat Gruff and I am off to the meadow to eat the sweet grass," he said.

"Oh, no, you are not! I am going to gobble you up!" cried the troll and he reared up from his hiding place.

"You don't want to do that," replied the Billy Goat. "You should wait for my big brother."

So the troll let the middle-sized Billy Goat past and waited for the largest Billy Goat Gruff to pass by. Soon he came trotting over the bridge, trip, trap, trip, trap

"Who is that trip-trapping over my bridge?" roared the angry troll. "I am going to eat you all up!" But the biggest Billy Goat Gruff did not look at all afraid. He pawed the rickety wooden bridge with his strong hooves, lowered his head and then the troll suddenly spotted his two sharp horns — but it was too late! The big Billy Goat Gruff thundered towards him and his mighty horns butted the troll high into the air. He landed in the river with a loud splash and was never seen again. And the Three Billy Goats Gruff lived happily ever after in their lush meadow and grew very fat indeed!

THE BEAR
WILL HAVE TO GO

While Lucy slept in the shade of a tree, Cuthbert went for a walk into the woods and was soon quite lost. He had no idea which way was back, so he sat down and thought about what to do next.

When Lucy awoke, she looked around in surprise. Her teddy bear, Cuthbert, was missing. She thought someone had taken him, for she didn't know that when people are asleep their teddy bears like to go walking.

"Cuthbert!" she called. "Cuthbert, where are you?"

He wasn't very far away. Lucy soon found him sniffing at a clump of moss.

"There you are!" she sighed. "I thought I'd lost you. Where's your waistcoat?"

In fact, Lucy really had lost Cuthbert, for the bear she was now taking home was not a teddy bear at all, but a real baby bear cub! As they ran back through the woods, the bear in Lucy's arms kept very still. He stared straight ahead without blinking, and tried not to sneeze. Soon they were back in Lucy's bedroom. Lucy flung the bear on her bed, then went to run a bath.

"Time to escape!" thought the bear. He slid off the bed, pulling the covers after him. He ran over to the window and tried to climb up the curtains. They tore down and tumbled to a heap on the floor. Just then Lucy's mother came into the room. The bear froze. Then Lucy appeared.

"Look at this mess," said Lucy's mother. "You've been playing with that bear again. Please tidy up."

Lucy had no idea how her room had got in such a mess, but she tidied up, took the bear into the bathroom and put him on the edge of the tub.

"Don't fall in," she said, and went to fetch a towel. The bear jumped into the tub with a great splash. He waved his paws wildly sending sprays of soapy water across the room. When he heard footsteps, he froze and floated on his back in the water as if nothing was wrong. It was Lucy, followed by her mother. "Oh, Lucy! What a mess!"

"Cuthbert must have fallen in," cried Lucy, rubbing his wet fur with a towel.

"A teddy bear couldn't make all this mess on its own," said Lucy's mother. "Please clean it up."

Lucy looked carefully at Cuthbert. Something was different about him, but she just couldn't work out what it was.

That night, while Lucy slept, the bear tip-toed downstairs. He needed to get back to the woods where he belonged, but he was hungry. In the kitchen he found lots of food, and he had a feast.

When Lucy came down for a glass of milk she found him with food all over his paws. The bear froze. Then her mother appeared in the doorway.

"This is the last straw, Lucy," said her mother, crossly. "You have been very naughty today, and every time something happens you've got that bear with you. If there is any more bad behaviour, the bear will have to go."

When her mother had gone back upstairs, Lucy looked carefully at the bear.

"You're not Cuthbert are you?" she said. The bear looked back at her and blinked. Lucy gasped. "You're a real bear!"

Now all the mess made sense! Lucy could
hardly believe she had made such a mistake. She
stroked the bear gently and he licked her finger.

"I'd better get you back to the woods before
there's any more trouble," she said. "And I'd
better try to find the real Cuthbert."

So early next morning, before her parents were
awake, she crept out of the house carrying the
bear. Out in the woods she put the bear on the
ground. He licked her hand and padded away.

Lucy was sad to see the little bear go. She wiped a tear from her eye as she turned away... and there at the foot of a tree sat her teddy bear, Cuthbert! Lucy picked him up and hugged him.

"Where have you been?" she asked. "You'll never guess the trouble I've been in. What have you been doing all night?"

Cuthbert said nothing. He just smiled. What had he been doing all night? Well, that's another story!

TEA WITH THE QUEEN

Teddy bear, teddy bear,
Where have you been?
I've been up to London to visit the queen!

I went to her palace,
And knocked at the gate,
And one of her soldiers said, please would I wait?

Then one of her footmen,
All dressed in red,
Led me inside, saying, step this way, Ted!

And there in a huge room,
High on her throne,
Sat the poor queen, taking tea all alone.

She said, how delightful,
Sit down, fill your tum!
And soon we were chattering just like old chums!

And when time came to leave,
She shook hands and then,
She said, come back soon, we must do it again!

THE COW WHO
JUMPED OVER THE MOON

Boing, boing, boing! Bouncy Bunny kicked up her heels and bounded across the field.

"I can bounce high in the air, watch me!" she called to the other animals on the farm. Her fluffy white tail bobbed up and down.

"Very good!" said Silly Sheep, who was easily impressed.

"Yes, very good," said Swift, the sheepdog. "But not as good as me. I can jump right over the gate.

With that, he leapt over the gate and into the field.

"Amazing!" said Silly Sheep.

"Yes, amazing," said Harry Horse, with a flick of his mane. "But not as amazing as me. I can jump right over that hedge. Watch me!" And with that, he galloped around the field, then leapt high into the air, and sailed over the tall hedge.

"Unbelievable!" said Silly Sheep.

"Yes, unbelievable," said Daisy, the cow, chewing lazily on a clump of grass. "But not as unbelievable as me. I can jump right over the moon!"

"Well, I'm afraid that is unbelievable, Daisy," said Harry Horse. "No one can jump over the moon. That's just a fairy story."

"Well, I can," said Daisy, stubbornly. "And I can prove it! You can watch me do it if you like!"

The other animals all agreed that they would very much like to see Daisy jump over the moon.

"Meet me here in the field tonight, then," said Daisy to them. "When the moon is full, and the stars are shining bright."

So that night, when the moon had risen high up in the sky, the excited animals gathered together in the field. The rest of the animals from the farm came along too, for word had soon spread that Daisy the cow was going to jump over the moon, and they were all eager to watch.

"Come along then, Daisy," said Swift, the sheepdog, as the animals waited impatiently. "Are you going to show us how you can jump over the moon, or not?"

All the animals laughed, as they thought that Daisy was just boasting, and that she would not really be able to do it.

"Yes, I am going to show you," said Daisy, "but first of all, you will have to come with me. This isn't the right spot." Daisy led the animals across the field, to the far side, where a little stream ran along the edge of the field, separating it from the dark woods on the other side.

"Now, stand back everyone, and give me some room," said Daisy. The animals did as they were asked, and watched Daisy with anticipation, giggling nervously. Whatever was she going to do?

Daisy trotted back to the middle of the field, then ran towards the stream at a great speed.

At the last moment, she sprang into the air, and sailed across the stream, landing safely on the other side.

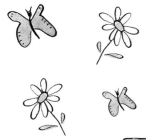

"I did it!" cried Daisy. "Aren't you going to clap, then?" The other animals looked at each other in confusion.

"But you only jumped over the stream!" said Harry Horse, puzzled.

"Come and take a closer look," called Daisy, still on the far side. The animals gathered close to

the water's edge. They looked down, and there reflected in the water shimmered the great full moon! How the animals laughed when they realised Daisy had tricked them.

"See?" said Daisy. "I really can jump over the moon!" And just to prove it, she jumped back to the field again. The animals all clapped and cheered.

"That was a very good trick!" said Swift.

"Amazing!" said Silly Sheep. "Could someone explain it to me again, please?"

LITTLE SHEEP

Little Sheep couldn't sleep,
Not a wink, not a peep!
Tossing, turning, all night through,
What was poor Little Sheep to do?

Owl came by, old and wise,
Said, "Silly sheep, use your eyes –
You're lying in a field of sheep,
Try counting them to help you sleep!"

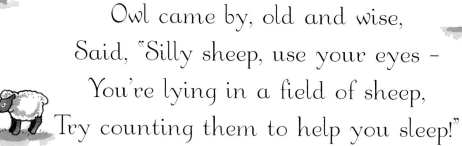

"Seven, four, thirteen, ten –
That's not right, I'll start again..."
Till daylight came, awake he lay
And vowed he'd learn to count next day!

GIRAFFE'S SONG

It's wonderful having a long neck,
That reaches right up to the sky,
You can nibble the leaves on the treetops,
And smile at the birds flying by.

It's wonderful having a long neck,
You can see for miles around,
You always know just where
your friends are,
And where the best food can be found.

It's wonderful having a long neck,
Although, I'm not meaning to gloat.
For there's one time that I really curse it,
And that's when I get a sore throat!

I Am a Music Man

LEADER: I am a music man,
I come from far away,
And I can play.

ALL: What can you play?

LEADER: I play piano.

ALL: Pia, pia, piano, piano, piano,
Pia, pia, piano, pia, piano.

LEADER: I am a music man,
I come from far away,
And I can play.

ALL: What can you play?

LEADER: I play the big drum.

ALL: Boomdi, boomdi, boomdi boom,
Boomdi boom, boomdi boom,
Boomdi, boomdi, boomdi boom,
Boomdi, boomdi boom.
Pia, pia, piano, piano, piano,
Pia, pia, piano, pia, piano.

364

LEADER: I am a music man,
I come from far away,
And I can play.

ALL: What can you play?

LEADER: I play the trumpet.

ALL: Tooti, tooti, tooti, toot,
Tooti, toot, tooti, toot,
Tooti, tooti, tooti, toot,
Tooti, tooti, toot.

Boomdi, boomdi, boomdi boom,
Boomdi boom, boomdi boom,
Boomdi, boomdi, boomdi boom,
Boomdi, boomdi boom.

Pia, pia, piano, piano, piano,
Pia, pia, piano, pia, piano.

Pretend to play each instrument in turn

365

Ring-A-Ring O'Roses

Ring-a-ring o'roses,
A pocket full of posies,
A-tishoo! A-tishoo!
We all fall down!

Dance around in a ring, pretend to sneeze, then fall down on the floor

Pop Goes the Weasel

Half a pound of tu'penny rice,
Half a pound of treacle.
That's the way the money goes,
POP! Goes the weasel.

A bouncing on the knee rhyme, with an extra big bounce on the "Pop!"

I Hear Thunder

(To the tune of Frère Jacques)

I hear thunder,
I hear thunder,
Oh! Don't you?
Oh! Don't you?

Pitter, patter raindrops,
Pitter, patter raindrops,
I'm wet through,
I'm wet through.

Pretend to listen

Flutter hands like rain

Wrap arms around body

I HEAR THUNDER...

PITTER, PATTER RAINDROPS

I'M WET THROUGH

Hurry up the sunshine,
Hurry up the sunshine,
I'll soon dry,
I'll soon dry.

I see blue skies,
I see blue skies,
Way up high,
Way up high.

Point up to sky

WAY UP HIGH

Circle hands in front of chest

HURRY UP THE SUNSHINE

Pretend to shake hands dry

I'LL SOON DRY

Simple Simon

Simple Simon met a pieman
Going to the fair,
Says Simple Simon to the pieman
"Let me taste your ware."
Says the pieman to Simple Simon,
"Show me first your penny."
Says Simple Simon to the pieman,
"Indeed I have not any."

Simple Simon went a-fishing
For to catch a whale;
But all the water he had got
Was in his mother's pail.

The Owl and the Pussy-cat

The Owl and the Pussy-cat went to sea

In a beautiful pea-green boat,

They took some honey, and plenty of money,

Wrapped up in a five-pound note.

The Owl looked up to the stars above,

And sang to a small guitar,

"O lovely Pussy! O Pussy, my love,

What a beautiful Pussy you are,

You are, you are!

What a beautiful Pussy you are!"

Pussy said to the Owl, "You elegant fowl!

How charmingly sweet you sing!

"O let us be married! Too long we have tarried:

But what shall we do for a ring?"

They sailed away, for a year and a day,

To the land where the Bong-tree grows,

And there in a wood a Piggy-wig stood,

With a ring at the end of his nose,

His nose, his nose,

With a ring at the end of his nose.

"Dear Pig, are you willing to sell for one shilling
Your ring?" Said the Piggy, "I will."
So they took it away, and were married next day
By the Turkey who lives on the hill.

They dined on mince, and slices of quince,
Which they ate with a runcible spoon;
And hand in hand, on the edge of the sand,
They danced by the light of the moon,
The moon, the moon,
They danced by the light of the moon.

BEARS AHOY

One summer's day, three little boys went for a picnic by the bank of a river. They took with them their swimming things, some cheese and tomato sandwiches and, of course, their teddy bears.

When they arrived, they found a small boat tied to a tree. The boys climbed on board, taking their teddies with them, and had a great game of pirates. The boys pretended to walk the plank, and soon they were all splashing about, playing and swimming in the river. They chased each other through the shallow water, and disappeared along the river and out of sight.

Now, the three bears left on board the boat did not get on very well together. Oscar was a small, honey-colored bear. He was good friends with Mabel, who had shaggy brown fur, but neither of them liked Toby. He was bigger than they were and he was a bully. He was always growling at the other bears and telling them what to do.

As soon as the boys were out of sight, Toby leapt to his feet. The boat rocked. Oscar and Mabel begged him to sit down.

"I'm a fearless sailor," cried Toby. "I've sailed the seven seas and now I'm going to sail them again." He untied the boat, and pushed it away from the bank. The boat lurched from side to side.

"Come on, crew. Look lively!" shouted Toby. "Do as I say or I'll make you walk the plank." Now that it was untied, the little blue boat began to drift. It turned sideways gently, then caught the main current and began to gather speed.

"Toby!" cried Oscar. "We're moving!"

"Of course we are, you big softie," growled Toby. "We're bold and fearless pirates on the high seas."

Oscar and Mabel clung together in fright, as the little boat sailed down the river, past fields and houses. "Help!" they shouted. "Toby, make it stop!" But Toby was having a great time.

"Ha, ha," shouted Toby. "This is the life!"

Oscar glanced over the side. He wished he hadn't. The sight of everything passing by so quickly made him feel seasick.

"Look out, Toby!" he cried. "We're going to hit the bank. Steer it away."

But Toby did nothing. The boat hit the bank with a thump and Toby fell forward. The boat swung round and headed for the middle of the river once more.

"Toby!" shouted Mabel. "Save us!"

But Toby was sitting in the bottom of the boat, rubbing a big bump on his head.

"I can't. I don't know how to sail a boat," he whimpered, feebly. He hid his face in his paws and began to cry. The boat zig-zagged on down the river, with the little bears clinging on to the sides in fright. In time, the river became wider and they could hear the cry of seagulls.

"Oh, Toby," cried Mabel. "We're heading for the sea. Do something!"

"Nobody likes me," wailed Toby. "Now we're going to sink to the bottom of the sea, and you won't like me either!"

Oscar wasn't listening. He had found a rope hanging from the sail. "Let's put the sail up and see if it will blow us to shore," he said.

"We'll be blown out to sea," wailed Toby, but Oscar ignored him, and carried on. The wind filled the sail and the little boat started moving forward. They sailed right across the bay to the far side, and blew up on to the beach.

"Oh, Oscar, you are a hero!" sighed Mabel, hugging him tight. "You saved us!"

Imagine the bears' surprise to see the three little boys running towards them along the beach – they had gone to find the coastguard and raise the alarm. There were hugs and kisses all round when they found the bears safe and sound. And you can be sure that from that day on, Toby was a much wiser and kinder bear, and he never bullied the others again.

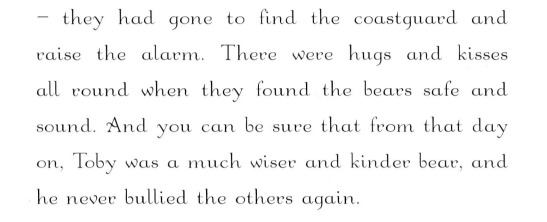